C000124538

THE ISLAND STORM

Getaway Bay, Book 6

ELANA JOHNSON

Copyright © 2021 by Elana Johnson

All rights reserved.

No part of this book may be reproduced in any form or by any electronic or mechanical means, including information storage and retrieval systems, without written permission from the author, except for the use of brief quotations in a book review.

ISBN-13: 978-1-63876-008-5

Chapter One

L isa Ashford tucked her hair behind her ear and looked down at her to-do list. Nearly everything had been crossed off, as she'd been bustling around the office for the past several hours.

Only one item remained, and she'd been putting it off for a reason. But the company's spring barbecue sat only hours away now, and someone needed to approach Hope for the keys to the van so they could get all the food loaded up.

Shannon had organized the company party for a couple of years now, but this new spring barbecue had fallen to Lisa, as she had the fewest brides getting married this summer and fall. Organizing a barbecue played right to her strengths, and she hadn't minded calling around to find the perfect location—the private pool on the twenty-sixth floor at the Sweet Breeze Resort and Spa, thank you very much—ordering food, making invitations, and designing a theme.

In fact, all of that made Lisa's soul sing. But getting budget approvals from Hope had been the bane of her party planning, and the owner of Your Tidal Forever ruthlessly questioned everyone who wanted to use one of the company vans as if they'd be taking the ugly mom-vehicles on joyrides.

A flash of a smile touched Lisa's lips at the same time she wished she owned a mom-vehicle. Then she'd be a mother, something she wanted very badly. But her dating luck seemed to have run out years ago, despite everyone's reassurances that she'd find the perfect guy for her.

She'd tried the singles app that had matched a lot of people on the island of Getaway Bay in recent years, but she only found more guys looking for a good time or unwilling to commit. Or maybe they didn't like blondes. Whatever it was, she'd deleted her profile as a New Year's resolution, and she'd resorted to more traditional methods of finding a man.

Which meant she hadn't been out with anyone in four months. The only men she came in contact with were already married or about to be. Didn't leave her much room to get someone's number.

Steeling herself, she tugged down the hem of her blouse and clicked her way down the hall to Hope's office. The woman had been working less and less the past few months, and Lisa actually wondered if she was getting ready to sell the company. Maybe she was sick.

Something. Hope wasn't the same as she'd been, Lisa knew that.

Shannon already sat in her office, and Lisa was glad for the buffer. "Excuse me, Hope?" she asked. "We've got everything ready for the barbecue tonight, and I just need keys to the van to get things loaded up."

"Sure." Hope gave her a weary smile and opened one of her desk drawers. "Just one set?"

"Yes," she said as Shannon rose from her chair. She took the keys and handed them to Lisa as she joined her near the door.

"Have fun," Hope said, looking back down at her appointment book.

"Are you not coming?" Lisa asked, true surprise moving through her.

"I am," Hope said, glancing up again. "But I'll be a little late."

"Oh, okay." Lisa didn't know what else to say. She'd worked with Hope for a decade now, and she would've liked to have been better friends with her boss. But she wasn't, and she had the keys, so she turned and left the office.

Shannon came right on her heels, murmuring, "She and Aiden are having some problems."

Instant regret about her somewhat poisonous thoughts hit Lisa. "Oh, that's too bad." She paused at the door of Shannon's office. "You're still helping me with the setup, right?"

"Yes, let me put on my jeans and change my shoes."

Lisa wished she'd thought that far ahead. Hope liked everyone in the office to be dressed to the nines, and the dress code was actually something Lisa liked. She loved cute dresses and skirts, brightly colored tops, shoes with jewels on them, and jewelry. Oh, the jewelry. She probably owned a hundred bangles, and she was always looking for more.

Her shoes today were wedges, and she'd be fine carrying in napkins wearing shoes like that. They did have ribbons, which made her happy. And besides, she'd just stop at the front desk and ask for the bell service to bring out a cart to load everything on to.

Several minutes later, she and Shannon filled the van with cases of soda, paper products, and decorations. The Happy Hamburger was providing all of the food, and they'd have their own people deliver it only fifteen minutes before the party began.

"Ready?" she asked as Shannon tossed in the last package of paper plates.

"So ready," she said. "This spring has been brutal, hasn't it?"

"Only for you," Lisa said.

"Losing Riley has been hard," Shannon said as she started for the passenger door. Lisa got behind the wheel and buckled her seatbelt, a wail of missing for her best friend pulling through her. If she'd known Shannon was talking about how brutal things were personally, then yes, this spring without Riley had been terrible.

"I know," she said, because Riley had left Your Tidal

Forever four months ago. Left Lisa to deal with her bad dates on her own. Left the island in favor of working as the manager for her boyfriend's band.

Lisa didn't blame her; if she had a rich, celebrity boyfriend who'd offered her a dream job, she would've taken it too.

She just missed her best friend. She had other friends at the office, of course. But they had boyfriends or husbands, and Lisa felt like she was suffering in silence.

She navigated the traffic in East Bay, finally getting on the one road that went over to Getaway Bay, where the resort was. After pulling into the valet circle, she let Sterling open her door, giving him a bright smile.

"Heya, Sterling," she said.

"Miss Lisa," he said, the tips of his ears turning bright red. She half-liked his reaction to her, and half-disliked it. She didn't want to intimidate men, and he'd never asked her out. Maybe she should just ask him.

"We're going to need one of your fancy carts," she said, still toying with the idea of leaving this party with a date. "And Howie from The Happy Hamburger is bringing our food in forty-five minutes."

"I've got it on the schedule," he said. "I'll call Paul for you." He stepped over to his podium and picked up the phone while Shannon opened the back of the van.

Lisa thought about picking up a package of plastic forks—she could carry *something* upstairs—when a man said, "Evening, ladies. Need some help?"

"Wow, that was fast," Lisa said, turning. She expected to see someone from the resort there, a cart at the ready.

She found Cal Lewiston.

Tall, broad, bearded Cal Lewiston.

Her breath caught and her pulse skipped. "Hey," she said, her thoughts moving from Sterling to Cal. "What are you doing here?"

"There's a barbecue tonight, right?" He looked puzzled as he met her eyes and then let his gaze slide behind her to the van.

"Yeah, but not for another hour," Lisa said, appreciating his stature, all those muscles…. Why hadn't she thought of him as a possible date? He owned his own carpentry business on the island, but Your Tidal Forever did a ton of contract work with him.

"Oh, well, I guess I'm early." He grinned at her, and that so wasn't fair. Maybe Lisa's brain had been fried because of all this party prep. Maybe she just hadn't seen Cal for a while. Maybe she was just so incredibly lonely, or she hadn't been out with a man in so long, or something, that she couldn't seem to look away from the handsome lines of his face. That strong nose, that square jaw, those deep, dark blue eyes.

The hair on his head and face was a lighter brown, and he ran one hand along his jaw in what appeared to be a nervous tic.

"All of this?" another man asked, and Lisa jumped. The real bellhop had just arrived, and thankfully, Shannon answered for her. She stepped out of the way as

Cal and Paul started loading everything from the back of the van onto a cart, and then they all rode up to the twenty-sixth floor together.

———

A COUPLE OF HOURS LATER, LISA STOOD TO THE SIDE OF the soda table, her third diet cola in her hand. The barbecue had been going well enough. The food had arrived. Everyone from Your Tidal Forever had too— including Hope and her husband Aiden. He worked as a photographer for the company, and Lisa didn't detect any strain between them.

People were changing into their swimming suits, but Lisa hadn't brought one of those either. In the next moment, the music started, just as Owen, the general manager here at Sweet Breeze, had assured her it would. *Six o'clock, on the dot*, she thought, glad everything was running smoothly.

Everyone seemed to have someone they were talking to, especially since plus-ones had been encouraged for this company party. As the seconds ticked by, Lisa felt more and more like disappearing. She, of course, had not invited anyone to come with her. Sure, she had a cousin somewhere on the island, but it wasn't like she was besties with her.

Both of her sisters lived on Oahu, and one was married and the other was probably on a hot date with her very serious boyfriend. She could call them, but they wouldn't be able to do anything. So Lisa was alone. Always alone.

Then her eyes caught on Cal.

He sat at a table by himself, a glass of bright pink lemonade in front of him. He hadn't brought a plus-one either. Without thinking, Lisa started toward him. With every step, her heartbeat pulsed faster and faster. What was she even going to say?

He lifted his drink to his lips and swallowed, the movement in his throat somehow making the temperature of Lisa's blood go up.

"Hey," she said when she arrived. The song switched to something slower, and she blurted the first thing that came to her mind. "Do you want to dance with me?"

Cal looked up, pure surprise in those gorgeous eyes. He didn't answer immediately, which only made Lisa more nervous. She reached for his drink and drained the last couple of swallows before setting it back on the table. "I promise not to step on your feet."

He tracked every movement, something playful sparking in his eyes. "All right," he said, standing up.

She wasn't sure if that was a good *all right* or a pity one. In this moment, it didn't matter. She wasn't going to stand on the sidelines during the social hour of this party. And she couldn't leave early.

"Great." She turned away from him, cursing herself for this dance invitation. What if the man had a girlfriend? Surely he did, because a male specimen as good-looking as him didn't stay single for long. Maybe he just hadn't invited her to this party. Maybe she'd had to work. So many maybe's, and Lisa actually wanted to turn off her brain.

"Watch out," someone called. Maybe Cal. Maybe not.

Lisa flinched, not really sure what she was supposed to watch out for. A basketball hit her in the hip, and she felt her leg buckle.

A cry came from her throat as she tipped, and she only had enough time to realize what was happening before she toppled right into the swimming pool.

Shock coursed through her, though the water wasn't cold, and she came up sputtering. Her hair. Her makeup. Her dangly earrings.

Her clothes.

Lisa sucked at the air, pure humiliation filling her, and filling her, and filling her. It was fine. She'd just get out of the pool and dry off somewhere no one would find her.

"You okay?" a man asked, and Lisa just nodded, still trying to catch her breath and hide at the same time.

"I got you," Cal said, reaching down and hauling her out of the pool as if she weighed nothing. "After all, you owe me a dance."

Chapter Two

"I might need a raincheck," Lisa said, making Cal Lewiston's nerves fray again.

He wouldn't follow through on a raincheck, and everything in him wanted to dance with this woman. Surprisingly.

Dripping wet or not, she was the most beautiful woman he'd encountered in a while. Truth be told, he hadn't even thought about asking a woman for a date in a very long time. A very, *very* long time.

"Let me get you a towel." He kept one hand on her elbow as he guided her over to the huge stack of towels in a bin near the gate. He hadn't brought his swimwear either. He'd been thinking about quietly slipping away from this party before Lisa had shown up and finished his drink and asked him to dance.

His daughter would be home in an hour, and Cal liked to be there when Sierra arrived. That way, he knew her boyfriend hadn't stayed for too long, and he knew what they were doing. Cal didn't like his fourteen-year-old daughter with a boyfriend at all. Sierra barely seemed capable of getting to school on time and finishing her homework at night, let alone managing a relationship with a boy two years older than her.

Or maybe that was just Cal who'd been having a hard time with his relationships. He only had the one with his daughter to worry about, and that was difficult enough.

Lisa Ashford said something about being fine, but Cal grabbed a towel and wrapped it around her shoulders anyway. She clutched the ends of it and looked up at him through her eyelashes, almost like she didn't want to commit to making true eye contact.

"Thank you," she said.

"Sure thing," he said, glad he still knew how to talk to a pretty woman. "The song is over, but we can still dance." The music coming from the speakers set high above the pool wasn't anything Cal had ever heard before, and it certainly wasn't something romantic he could dance to. Hold Lisa close. Smell that perfume.

Of course, now she radiated the scent of chlorine, and Cal felt a moment of pity for her.

"I'm going to go get dried off," she said, taking a step past him.

He wanted to get confirmation of a raincheck, but before he could say anything, the building shook. Everything went silent for a moment, and Cal's heart dropped to his toes and rebounded back to his chest.

"Was that an earthquake?" someone asked, and a few people moved over to the edge of the building. The wall there was much too high to see very much—Cal had already looked earlier. The building swayed slightly, and he seemed to remember reading about this building as it was under construction.

His eyes met Lisa's, and she looked afraid. "I think they built this building to sway a little in the wind," he said.

"It's not windy," she said just as the music from the speakers muted.

"All guests need to move immediately to the sixth floor and above," a man said over the public intercom. The words echoed down below Cal, clearly going out to everyone on the beach too. The most popular beach on the island.

"All people can take shelter in Sweet Breeze. Use the stairs. All elevators will be disabled. Everyone needs to get to the sixth floor or above."

A general cry rose up from the ground below, and Cal couldn't help moving to the wall as well. Lisa joined him, and they could see people scattering.

"It had to be an earthquake," Lisa said, and Cal immediately looked out to the ocean.

"And a tsunami warning," he said, almost a whisper. His blood ran cold.

Sierra.

She was supposed to be at the library with Travis. Where would they shelter? He reached for his phone and tapped to call his daughter, his heartbeat firing in his chest with the speed of an automatic rifle.

The line had rung once when tsunami siren started, filling the air with a chilling wail. "Let's get inside," he said, reaching for Lisa with his free hand and towing her away from the side of the building.

Everyone had the same idea, and Cal and Lisa joined the stream of people from Your Tidal Forever trying to get inside.

"Guests on the sixth floor and above, please open your rooms to those coming in from the beach. All restaurants, theaters, museums, and guest rooms should be cleared on floors one through five." The announcements continued, and Sierra didn't answer her phone.

Cal's panic doubled, and he quickly tapped out a message to his daughter. Tsunami. Get to high ground or above the fifth floor of a building. I'm at Sweet Breeze. Twenty-sixth floor. Where are you?

He sent the message, every cell in his body wailing. He couldn't lose his daughter too. Not after they'd both lost Jo. Desperation clogged his throat, and he stepped through the glass doors and into the main building right behind Lisa, tapping to call Sierra again.

"Dad," she said breathlessly before the phone had even rung.

"Where are you?" he asked.

"We're at the library," she said. "They're telling us to go to the roof."

Cal closed his eyes for a moment, everything going black. He couldn't think. "How many stories is the library?" He should know, he'd lived on the island of Getaway Bay his whole life. But he couldn't *think*.

"Four," she said. Clamoring came from her end of the line. Shouts.

"Stay with Travis," Cal said, his voice growing louder too. "I'm at Sweet Breeze. I'll come get you two as quickly as I can after the waves hit."

A roaring noise sounded behind him, and pure fear gripped his lungs. "I love you, coconut," he said, his voice choking.

"Dad, I love you," she said—and the line went dead.

Helpless, Cal shoved his phone in his pocket and twisted to look behind him. A few people still stood at the wall, and one pointed. The man turned, horror etched on his face. He ran toward the crowd still pushing to get in the building.

The water must've receded, which meant the tsunami was coming. That, or the man had seen the waves and realized the immensity of danger the whole island was in.

Please let Sierra and Travis get to the roof quickly, Cal prayed. Keep me safe. Help me find them as fast as possible.

"This way," he said, tugging on Lisa's hand to get her to go down a hallway. That would free up more room for more people to come in off the pool deck and get them away from the glass. Why everyone wanted to be in the lobby just outside the pool, he wasn't sure. He didn't want to see the tragedy about to happen.

Lisa shivered, and Cal put his arm around her, pressing her into a wall as they met a group of people that had come this way before them.

"It's okay," he said. "We're really high up."

"What if the building falls?" she asked.

Cal didn't want to answer that question. The anxiety in the air was almost to his breaking point, and he prayed again. *Jo, baby, watch over us.*

His late wife just had to protect Sierra. Cal couldn't lose her too.

Moments later, screams filled the air from those still down by the doors. A rush of people flowed down the hall toward them, and Cal braced himself, his fingers tightening along Lisa's upper arm.

"Here we go," he murmured, and the building shuddered again. It swayed wildly—at least in Cal's opinion—and he pressed one palm into the wall as a cry of fright from the others lifted up. He groaned and grunted, trying to find a solid place to stand.

It was a strange and scary feeling to have solidness beneath his feet and still be moving so much.

Everything quieted after only ten seconds.

"There could be residual waves," someone said.

"Stay put," another woman called.

Cal was glad no one had lost their heads. Everyone stayed still for several long minutes, and the building definitely moved a few more times. Nothing like the initial hit of the waves, and Cal could only hope that the roof of the library was high enough to protect his baby.

"All guests should stay where they are," the man on the intercom said. "Please, stay where you are."

Curiosity burned through Cal. He wanted to see how much water had come ashore. Needed to know. His fingers twitched, and his pulse beat too hard in his chest.

"Well, that wasn't the dance I was expecting," Lisa said beside him, and he moved his gaze to hers.

A chuckle started in his throat, and he kept it low— for her ears only. "No, definitely not."

She smiled at him. "Who's at the library?"

He swallowed, all the teasing and playfulness between them gone. He hadn't dated since Jo's death, so he'd never had to tell a woman about his daughter. "Uh, my daughter," he said.

Surprise entered Lisa's expression, though he wasn't sure why. No, he hardly knew her. But most people knew he'd been married with a family.

Your friends know that, he told himself. And Lisa just worked at the company that hired him to build altars and trellises. She didn't *know* him. They weren't friends.

Yet.

"Oh," she said. "How old is she?"

"Fourteen," he said. He didn't mean to sound so tired when he said it, but fourteen-year-old girls were a special breed of human. "She tests me sometimes," he said, as if Lisa had heard the weariness and asked about it. "But she's a good girl. She's with her boyfriend."

He pulled out his phone and started to text Sierra

again, hoping the cell phone towers had survived the waves. *We're okay here at the hotel*, he said. *How are you?*

The circle indicating the message had been sent spun and spun, and he looked up. "No service."

Lisa had her phone out too. "None for me either."

Pure frustration filled Cal. "I need to get to the library." Part of him didn't want to leave her alone either. He looked at his message again, still trying to go through. He'd used the pronoun *we*.

We're okay at the hotel.

He looked at Lisa again. "Would you come with me to make sure my daughter is okay?"

Warmth filled her expression. "Of course," she said. "And you can come with me to see if my little bulldog survived." She ducked her head then, but not before Cal saw the emotion there. The fear. The hope. The pain.

He threaded his fingers through hers and squeezed. "We'll find him."

"It's a her," Lisa said, her voice a touch higher than normal. "Her name is Suzy."

"My daughter's name is Sierra," Cal said, the same hope-fear-pain moving through him. But he couldn't disconnect. Not again.

When Jo had died, his head had felt disconnected from the rest of him. He'd get texts and mean to answer them, but he never did. Things needed to be done for the funeral, with the house, with Sierra, and without the help of his parents, he felt certain nothing would've been accomplished.

"We'll locate the humans first," he said. "Just as soon as they let us out of here." He peered over the heads of the people next to them, wondering how long it would take for Sweet Breeze to deem the area safe enough to let everyone leave.

Chapter Three

Lisa checked her phone again, noting that seventy-five minutes had passed since she and Cal had agreed to stick together after they were released from the hotel. She hadn't been able to send a text, and the irritation and frustration level on the twenty-sixth floor could be cut with a knife.

In fact, Lisa wouldn't be surprised if someone started freaking out any moment now. Or if she were that person. She'd moved down the hall to talk to Shannon and Charlotte, and then Hope, but there was nothing anyone could do until the powers-that-be said they could leave Sweet Breeze.

She migrated back to Cal, reaching his side several moments later. A sense of comfort she didn't understand moved through her. She was glad she wasn't alone. That she didn't have to go through this alone. That she didn't have to go home to her bungalow alone, or look for Suzy alone.

She smiled up at him. "It has to be soon, right?"

"I'm going to lose my mind," he said in the calmest voice imaginable. He shifted his feet and looked at his phone again, the only signs of his discomfort.

"Ladies and gentlemen, the area surrounding Sweet Breeze Resort and Spa has been deemed safe," a man said. Probably Owen. "We advise extreme caution for those wishing to leave. Please use the stairs, and please don't push or run."

"Let's go," Cal said, already inching away from the wall. Lisa grabbed onto his hand so they could stay together. Several long minutes later, they reached the stairwell and started down. The lower they moved, the more congested it got.

But finally, she followed Cal through a doorway to bright sunshine. *Odd*, she thought, looking up into the sky. For some reason, she expected it to be gray and foaming with clouds. But it wasn't. It was a regular day, as if nothing had happened.

There was water everywhere, and Lisa glanced down at her ribboned wedges. They were ruined, and she didn't even care.

She kept up with Cal as he headed for the parking garage, but it soon became clear there would be no driving.

"Six inches of water," he said, craning his neck to see above the crowd. "Let's walk." He guided them to the boardwalk, which ran from Getaway Bay, under the canopy of trees, to East Bay.

Everything felt surreal. People were yelling to one another. Or for one another. Fronds and garbage and debris lay everywhere. A woman bent over and picked up a towel laden with water and sand.

Lisa couldn't take everything in all at the same time, and her head spun. She stumbled, and Cal said, "Whoa. You okay?"

She was not okay, but she couldn't vocalize it. His arms came around her, enveloping her, steadying her.

"It's okay," he said. "It's just shock. Take a minute." They stood in the middle of the boardwalk, pure chaos around them, while she figured out how to breathe again. She kept her eyes pressed closed, and a sense of vertigo rotated through her.

When it finally passed, she stepped out of his arms. "Okay. I'm okay."

"You've never been in a tsunami?" he asked.

"No," she said. "It's been a long time since one hit the island."

"Yeah," he said. "Probably fifteen years, I suppose." He looked out toward the water, his face a hard mask of stone. He was still handsome, though, and when he looked at her again, his dark blue eyes sparked with lightning. "Are we okay to keep going?"

"Yes," she said, pushing away the sight of so much destruction. "Let's go find your daughter."

The walk to the library took twenty minutes, each

step becoming drier and drier. The water had definitely come up this far, but less of it. And it had already receded back out to the ocean, or gone into coves, streams, or lakes.

A group of people stood behind a roped off section on the front steps of the library, and Cal headed that way. "Sierra?" he called, joining a line of other adults. "She has to be here. These all look like minors."

A man stood at the front of the line, talking to people, but Lisa wasn't sure what he was saying. When she and Cal got close enough, she heard, "Everyone who was in the library is safe. There were no injuries and no deaths."

Cal's relief beside her emanated from him. "So where are they?" he asked, stretching up onto his toes to see better. "How can we find them?"

"We kept everyone here who couldn't get in touch with a parent or loved one. We're asking you for their names before we release them."

Cal settled back onto his feet and waited his turn, his agitation growing by the moment. Finally, he stepped up the man and said, "Sierra Lewiston and Travis Bear."

The man scanned his clipboard and said, "They're at the top of the steps."

Cal took Lisa's hand again and up they went. Her calves hurt, but she didn't care. The man was about to be reunited with his daughter. Sure enough, he called, "Sierra," let go of her hand, and bounded up the last few steps, sweeping a dark-haired girl into his arms.

"Daddy," she said, crying into his shoulder. Lisa stood there and watched, her heart filling and filling with… something. Emotion of some sort. It was touching to see and feel the love Cal had for his daughter.

He set her down and grabbed onto the boy next to her, holding him close too. "You haven't talked to your parents?" he asked.

"No service," Travis said.

"Let's go see if they're okay," Cal said, turning back to Lisa. He seemed to stall for a moment, as if he'd forgotten she was there.

She put a brave smile on her face anyway. She really didn't want to go home alone, and if she had to trek over to wherever Travis lived to find out about his parents first, she'd do it.

"Guys, this is a friend of mine from work," Cal said, his eyes shooting sparks at her. "Lisa Ashford. Lisa, my daughter, Sierra and her boyfriend, Travis."

"So nice to meet you both," Lisa said, employing her wedding planner voice. She shook their hands as if they'd come in for a consultation and looked back at Cal.

"We have to get over to Travis's place," he said. "I understand if you want to go on to your house first."

"I'm okay," she said, though her stomach quivered. What would she find at her house? She wasn't right on the beach, but her bungalow definitely sat closer to the shoreline than the library did. She'd definitely have water damage. The question was how much, and if Suzy had managed to stay safe.

"Okay," Cal said. "It's a couple of miles, yeah?"

"At least," Sierra said, dread filling her face. "Travis has a car."

"They wouldn't let us take our cars," Cal said. "But we can try here."

Travis led them to the back of the library, and there was a line of cars trying to get out of the parking lot. "I say we try," Cal said, and Lisa's feet rejoiced.

Covering the few miles from the library to Travis's house took thirty minutes, but Lisa wasn't complaining. She listened to Sierra and Travis recount what they'd seen. From the roof of the library, they could see the wall of water coming ashore.

"They told us to get down," Sierra said. "Brace our backs against the concrete. But we could see it, Dad." She sounded half awed and half horrified.

"I've been in a few tsunami's now," he said. "They're all different."

"This one didn't seem so bad," Sierra said. "Is it a bad one?"

Lisa looked around at the debris, the broken-off trees. Yes, it was bad.

"Not so much," Cal said. "The windows broke out at Sweet Breeze on the first and second floors, allowing the water to go through. And the library didn't even have standing water left."

"I heard someone say it went halfway up the first floor," Travis said, easing around another corner. There was definitely damage in this neighborhood, as the yards looked like someone had come through with a wood chipper and eaten everything in sight.

"I see my mom," he said, excitement filling his voice. He pulled up to a house where a woman stood in the front yard, picking up discarded foliage. Travis spilled from the car, saying, "Mom."

He ran toward her and hugged her. The woman looked like she was in complete shock, and Lisa stayed in the car while Sierra and Cal got out. She couldn't hear their conversation, but Sierra hugged the woman too, and Cal put his arm around her shoulders.

They went into the house without looking back, and foolishness hit Lisa in the chest. She should've gone inside too. Or just gone home herself. She felt like an imposition to these people whom she barely knew.

She studied her hands, beyond ready to be out of her wet clothes. But everything on the island was wet, and she wondered if she'd even be able to stay in her house that night.

The car door opened, and Cal got behind the wheel. "Travis said we can borrow his car," he said. "You want to come up front and tell me where you live?"

Her eyes burned, and she realized she'd started to cry a little. She swiped at her face, got out of the backseat, and joined Cal in the front. "I'm sorry," she said. "You have a family to take care of, and—"

"It's fine," he said. "I asked Sierra to stay here with Travis and his parents. We're going to check your house and then mine, and we'll figure out a safe, dry place for everyone to stay tonight."

"Their house isn't that place, is it?" Lisa asked.

Cal shook his head and put the car in drive. "No, they can't stay there until things dry out. Carpet will need to be replaced. And all the walls dried out. They might have to be replaced too." He sighed. "But hey, I'm a carpenter, and I'll have a lot of work now." He kicked a partial grin at her, and Lisa marveled at the optimism in him.

"I'm over on Straw Avenue," she said. "A couple of blocks behind the movie theater."

Cal maneuvered them in that direction, staying silent.

"Are you divorced?" Lisa asked, partly because she couldn't stand to be inside her own head anymore, and partly because she wanted to know more about this man.

"My wife died almost three years ago," he said without looking at her.

"Oh, I'm so sorry," Lisa said, another wave of emotion rolling over her. She looked out the passenger window and didn't ask another question.

"What about you?" he asked. "Divorced? Widowed? Never been married?"

"The last one," she said quietly.

"No kids?" he asked.

"No kids," she confirmed. "Turn up there where that stop sign…used to be."

Cal did, something squealing in the car as they went

around the corner. "Boyfriend?" he asked at the same time she said, "I'm the fourth one on the right."

She swung her attention toward him. "Boyfriend? You think I have a boyfriend?"

"I'm asking if you have one," he said.

"No," Lisa said. She'd asked him to dance. What did he think that was?

"Fourth one on the right," he said, pulling to a stop in front of her house. They both looked at it, and she knew she wouldn't be staying there tonight. "Looks like you got some damage."

"Yeah." Lisa knew there probably wasn't a house on the island that hadn't sustained some damage. Maybe the ones clear up on the bluff. "Let's go see what the extent of the damage is." She got out of the car, and Cal met her at the hood.

He took her hand in his, and while there certainly wasn't a crowd here to separate them, Lisa held on. Holding hands with this man felt nice, and she needed the comfort as she walked toward the house, praying with everything inside her that Suzy was safe and sound inside.

She heard a bark when she tested her weight on the bottom step, and her heart leapt. "That has to be her."

"Let's see," Cal said, moving ahead of her and up to the front door. He twisted the knob and opened the door, and Lisa's little French bulldog came darting outside.

She laughed as she scooped up the little dog, a bolt of happiness moving through her. Suzy's wet paws soaked into Lisa's clothes, and she glanced at the walls. The water here had gone up about six inches, which meant she'd be able to pack a bag of dry clothes and work toward getting back to normal.

Cal touched her arm and said, "I'm going to call Sweet Breeze. Did you want a room too?"

"Yes, please," she said. "I'll go get packed, and then we can check out your house."

Chapter Four

C al didn't like the confining space of a hotel room. He stood at the window overlooking the beach from the fourteenth floor, actually envious of the tourists for the first time in his life.

His phone rang, but he ignored it. He'd fielded a dozen phone calls from individuals, homeowners associations, and general contractors about helping to get homes habitable again.

But he first had to get his own house ready to live in again. Sierra didn't even have school, as it too had been hit with the tsunami. Everything on the island seemed to be holding its breath, while people scurried around, working, working, working like busy little ants.

Garbage lined the streets, though crews worked around the clock to clear the debris.

"I'm going down to the school again today," Sierra said when she came out of the bathroom. Cal turned from his view. His daughter reached for her wallet, a tiny little thing that only carried a couple of cards and a few folded bills.

"You have money for lunch?" he asked, pulling his wallet from his back pocket.

"They feed us down there, Dad." She smiled at him and walked toward him. He hugged her, glad his daughter liked such things. "I told you that yesterday."

"Right." He sighed. "I forgot. I have a lot going on."

"Yeah, how's the house coming?"

"I have all the wet stuff out," Cal said. "Everything's dry. I'm going to get it all pieced back together today. We should only be here one more night." He hoped. He sincerely hoped. But he knew not everyone had his skills, and that he still had plenty to do around the island to help others get back to their homes too.

"Sounds good," Sierra said. "Travis said his house is coming along too. They have a neighbor who's been helping. And the local churches have been mobilizing to help people who don't have family and stuff."

"Yeah, I've heard that," Cal said. "As soon as our house is done, Sea, I'll take a job with an HOA to help out."

"I know, Dad." She smiled again and tucked her hair behind her ear. "I'll see you tonight, okay?"

"Love you," he said as she twisted the deadbolt to leave. "Be safe. Call me if anything happens."

"I will, Dad," she said, completing their daily parting

ritual. And then she was gone, the heavy hotel door slamming closed behind her.

Cal sighed, replaced his wallet in his pocket, and looked at his phone. He didn't recognize the number, but it had called more than once. Taking a chance, he called them back, only to get a chipper woman who said, "Thanks for calling me back, Mister Lewiston."

"I'm not sure who you are," he said, checking his pocket for his keys.

He followed his daughter out the door as the woman said, "I'm Hailey West, and I'm the manager for the Avenues homeowners association. We have quite a few residents here who need help with their homes, and I've been told you're the guy for the job."

Cal appreciated whoever had recommended him. "I can't start until Thursday," he said, giving himself two more days to finish his own house. He'd get all the walls done today, and he and Sierra could do the texturing and painting tomorrow. Then he'd be ready for another job.

"Thursday is great," Hailey said. "I wasn't expecting you to say yes." She trilled out a light laugh. "Our residents will be so happy." She cleared her throat. "I'd love it if you could come by today or tomorrow and do a quick walk-through, get a scope on the project, and give me a bid."

"Sure," he said. "Would right now work? I'm just headed out for the day."

"Of course," she said. "Let me give you the address for the office." She did, and Cal used the obligatory hotel pen and pad of paper to jot it down. "Be there in a few minutes," he said just as the elevator arrived. Good thing too, because there wasn't great reception in these Sweet Breeze elevators.

He didn't need his app to navigate his way to the office for the Avenues. He'd grown up and lived his entire life on the island, and he knew where to turn to get to the right street without all the stop signs that would lead him over to the Avenues in East Bay.

He glanced down Straw Avenue as he went past it, his heartbeat thumping out a few extra beats. Lisa's house was the fourth one down that street, and he realized that if he took this job, he could be the one working on her house.

He hadn't seen her since they'd checked in together, though he knew what room she was in. She knew his room number. But they hadn't exchanged phone numbers, and she was probably just as busy as he'd been, trying to manage her job with the cleanup process of her home.

He parked in one of the four spaces outside the office, the other few filled with Dumpsters that seemed to still have space in them. He cast them a long look before going inside, where a blonde woman rose from a desk.

"Cal Lewiston," she said, her voice bright and a plastic smile on her face. "Thank you for coming." She grabbed a map from her desk. "We can head right out. I'll show you what we're dealing with here." She clicked toward him in her high heels, and Cal held the door open for her.

She got behind the wheel of a golf cart, and he joined her. "We have eight avenues here," she said. "Many of the houses are owned by their occupants, and we have a lot of singles here, trying to manage their day jobs and their repairs, as well as several elderly couples who need a lot of help."

"All right," Cal said, and he opened a note app on his phone. "Let's go through them."

Hailey was nothing if not efficient, and she led him up and down the streets, knocked on doors, and charmed her way into damaged homes like she'd been born to do it. An hour later, he sat across from her desk, his head spinning.

"This is huge job," he said, glancing up from his notes. "I've only got four guys on my crew."

"Five of you is five more than we currently have," Hailey said with her professional smile. "What would your fee be? And I realize you've only just seen things here, but a timeline would be helpful as well."

Cal sighed and looked down at his phone again. "We'd prioritize the homes," he said. "Start with the ones that are still wet and need sheetrock ripped out and flooring pulled up." His brain moved through the timeline for that. Five guys. One of his men could probably do a house in a single day.

"So there are seventeen homes that need demo still," he said. "That's four days right there. Everything has to be bone dry to seal it up, so if we set up dryers—assuming we can get any—in the homes that are already pulled out, they'll be dry after the four days we need for demo. So that's five days...." He let his voice hang there.

Then they'd need supplies. Manpower to hang sheetrock and rebuild studs, if they were too wet. Flooring and people to do that labor.

"I could probably have your whole community put back together in three weeks," he said.

"You don't have other projects going on?" Hailey asked, a measure of surprise in her voice.

"I did," he said. "But all new construction has been put on hold while things get back to normal." He gave her a smile of his own, wondering if she could see the exhaustion in it.

"Very well. Three weeks," she said. "And the fee?"

"Three weeks of work, and supplies and equipment rental...." He swiped over to his calculator. "Forty thousand."

Hailey blinked, and he wasn't sure what was running through her mind. She glanced away and did some tapping on her own phone. "That's a fee of seven hundred and eighty dollars per resident," she said. "And our HOA board approved fees up to one thousand dollars."

"Great," Cal said, starting to stand. "You get the paperwork—"

"You should bid fifty-one thousand," she said, rising.

"Why?" Cal straightened, confused.

"Because that's one thousand dollars per resident," she said.

"Not all the homes need equal work," he said. "What about the one that's already dry and just needs the sheetrock and finishing?"

"The residents all voted to share the cost." She beamed at him. "We're a real community here."

"Do you live here?" he asked.

"Yes," she said. "I'm on Hamantu Avenue."

Cal smiled at her, knocking on her desk. "Great. But the fee is still just forty thousand." He turned to walk out. "Get me the paperwork, and I'll get my guys here on Thursday morning."

"Thank you," Hailey called after him, and Cal stepped outside. The blue sky above didn't seem to know that a tsunami had ripped apart homes and lives only four days ago. He sighed, his thoughts moving to Lisa again.

He'd get to work on her house, and he'd make sure he assigned himself to the fourth house on the right on Straw Avenue.

————

THURSDAY MORNING, HE GOT ANOTHER MAP FROM Hailey, this one blank, with only numbers on each of the lots. His eyes moved to Straw Avenue, and he said, "All right, guys. David, you take zone one." He continued assigning out the zones to each of his crew, making sure he got zone three, where Straw Avenue sat.

"Cody, you have three of the worst houses in your zone, so Adam, will you go with him today? Maybe see if you two can get those three houses done today. We have seventeen to do in three days, and that will put us one ahead."

"We'll do our best," Adam said.

"Marcos," Cal said, "You only have one house in your zone, so let's get it done today, and then we'll team up to get everything cleared out."

"How many dryers did we get?" Adam asked.

"Six," Cal said with a sigh. "And I almost had to give a kidney to get them." He indicated the back of his truck. "But we've got them, and we'll put them in whatever we can get done today. Find out if the residents have fans too." Most people in Hawaii did, and while a regular fan from a big box store wasn't the same as an industrial drying fan, it was better than nothing.

The crew broke up, each taking the supplies they needed and loading into their trucks. Cal watched them fan out, and then he got behind the wheel of his truck and drove over to Straw Avenue.

Lisa's house was one that hadn't been demolished yet, and he was starting on it as soon as he set up the dryers on the house at the end of the street from hers. With that done, he pulled into her driveway, his heartbeat pounding when he parked behind a white convertible.

He wasn't sure what she drove, but that seemed like a car that would fit her.

He climbed the steps and knocked on the door, only to have a cry come from inside. "Lisa?" he asked as he opened the door without waiting to be invited in.

He found her balancing in the hallway, one hand pressed against the wall as she held up her foot. Blood dripped to the bare wood floor below.

"What happened?" he asked, striding forward.

"I stepped on a nail," she said, lifting her brilliant blue eyes to meet his. "I managed to get some of the flooring up last night and look what I get."

Cal found her the sexiest woman he'd laid eyes on since his wife had died. And that was really saying something. Something big.

"Let me help you," he said when he reached her. He couldn't help smiling at her, and she smiled back. "And you know, this doesn't count as the dance."

She giggled, tucked her loose curls behind her ear, and looked up at him through those lashes.

"And I should totally get your number," Cal said, some of his previous flirting skills coming back to him in that moment. "That way, when you find yourself in another jam, you can call me."

"Oh, is that all you want my number for? Seems like *I* should get *your* number. You don't need mine."

Cal grinned at her, leaning closer though she was still steadily dripping blood onto her subfloor. "Lisa, if you want my number, it's yours."

Chapter Five

Lisa enjoyed the touch of Cal's fingers on her foot. Who knew the foot had so many nerve endings? Lisa didn't—unless the way her heels made her feet ache counted. Which it probably did.

"I think that's it," he said, his voice as low and powerful as it had been when he'd been panicked and talking to his daughter during the tsunami.

That silly tsunami.

Hope had closed Your Tidal Forever for the time being, but Lisa would honestly rather go to work. She couldn't rip up flooring and tear down wet sheetrock by herself. Since everyone around her had the same problems, and their own houses to fix, she hadn't been able to find much help.

Until now.

"What are you doing here?" she asked.

"Your HOA hired my crew to get everyone back up and running." He cocked a grin at her. "And I'm starting with your place."

An electric charge filled Lisa's whole body, and she had the strangest desire to duck her head and tuck her hair. Again.

So she refrained from doing that. The man had asked for her number, and she wasn't letting him leave here without it. In fact, if she could help it, she'd be leaving here *with him*.

"You're still at the hotel, right?" she asked.

"Actually, no," he said. "Sierra and I went home yesterday. She's finishing the painting today."

"Wow." Lisa glanced around, as her house still looked like a war zone. Fine, maybe not a war zone. She put dishes away, and she'd managed to pull up some of the flooring. It had been really hard though, and her shoulder still ached from where she'd ripped up the panel near the front door.

"Don't worry," he said. "I'll get your house back to normal in no time." He stood up, taking his beautiful presence with him. "So today, I'm going to do all the demo. It'll look worse when the day ends, but seriously, don't worry. It has to be torn apart in order to put it back together."

"I can help," Lisa said, and she would've called in "sick" to work had she been required to go into the office.

"All right," he said in that easy way of his. She

couldn't believe she hadn't gotten his number days ago, when they'd checked into the Sweet Breeze together. But the line had been an hour long by the time they'd checked his house, collected his daughter and Travis's family, and she'd honestly collapsed onto the hotel bed when she'd reached the eleventh floor.

She loved the hotel, and they'd gotten everything on floors three and above up and running the very next day. Their room service wasn't operational yet, as the kitchen was on the first floor, and they were having some electrical problems down there.

But there were three restaurants on the fourth floor, and everyone seemed to be getting fed. The most important part of the hotel, in Lisa's opinion, was the coffee shop on the fifth floor—and she wasn't the only one lining up at all hours of the day.

But she'd gotten her car from the parking lot at Your Tidal Forever, and thankfully, there had been no water damage to it. It had been banged around with a few other cars in the lot, but it still ran, and she'd been able to drive from her house to the hotel and back.

Technically, she could sleep at her house, but all citizens had been warned about mold spores, so she'd opted to stay at the resort with her French bulldog until everything was deemed safe.

"Do you have a fan?" Cal asked, bringing her back to her kitchen.

"Yes," she said. "Two, actually."

"I have one industrial one," he said. "We'll find the wettest spot and put that one there. We'll use yours in other key spots."

"Okay," she said, standing up and testing her weight on her injured foot. "Not bad, Doctor Lewiston."

That got him to laugh, and Lisa sure liked the sound of it.

"I'll go get my tools and everything. Be right back."

"I'll make more coffee."

"Ah, you know my love language." And with that, he walked away, deftly avoiding the exposed nails in the hallway that led to the front door.

"Love language," she repeated to herself. The man probably had no idea what he did to her pulse. The lingering scent of his cologne entered her nose as she hobbled over to the counter and poured the old coffee down the sink.

She knew the moment he re-entered the house, and not only because of the clomping of his work boots. He had a presence and a charisma that vibrated in her chest, and she wanted to be near him a lot more.

"Okay, how are you with a hammer?" he asked.

"Uh." She turned around, a bit of trepidation filtering through her. "I'm more of an online calendar type of woman."

"It's not too hard," he said. "I'm going to use my moisture detector to find the line where your sheetrock moves from dry to wet, and I'll cut a line in the wall. You pound out everything below it."

"Pound out?" she asked, taking the hammer from him. The smooth, black handle indicated that this tool was well-used, and Lisa felt like she'd knock herself unconscious before lunchtime.

"Yes," he said slowly. "Pound it all out. Rip it down. Throw it in the bin." He indicated the big blue bin behind him. "Do you have gloves?"

"Gardening gloves," she said. "Do those count?"

"No," he said with a smile. "I've got a spare pair." He took them from his back pocket and extended them toward her.

Lisa took them, looking down at the masculine, leather gloves that would drown her fingers.

"Pound it out," he said, turning in a full circle. "I'll start by the front door. You can follow me around after that."

"Okay." She put the gloves on the counter and finished making the coffee before joining him in the hallway again. "I should put shoes on."

"Good idea," he said, and she retreated to her bedroom to put on the proper footwear. Back in the hallway, she found him almost to the corner. "It's about a foot up now. Water seeps." He didn't look at her but continued looking at his meter and cutting a line in the wall with a utility knife.

He reached the corner and straightened. "You could just watch."

She jumped, because she'd just been caught staring at this fine, male specimen in her house. "I'm going to try to pound it out," she said, smiling at him and heading into the kitchen for the hammer.

The weight of it in her hand felt a little foreign, as she usually didn't lift more than a pen. Or a package of creamy, glossy stationery.

Swinging a hammer couldn't be that much harder than laying out the perfect spread of wedding cakes for a bridezilla to taste. Could it?

She reached the front door and found the cut line in the wall. "Okay," she muttered under her breath. "Here we go." She swung the hammer, but it barely made a dent in the wall.

"Harder," Cal said, and Lisa twisted to find him watching her this time. A sly smile touched those lips, and fire danced in those eyes, making them lighter than she'd seen them before.

Harder, she thought, cocking the hammer back and hitting the wall. A piece of it broke in, right where he'd cut the line in the wall. A squeal came out of her mouth as disbelief coursed through her. "I broke the wall."

Cal chuckled and clunked his way toward her. "You sure did. And you'll have to kind of tear it off the stud here." He yanked on the edge of the sheetrock, and a huge chunk of it tore off. Lisa was pretty sure she wouldn't be able to do that, but she wasn't going to let him outshine her.

She reached for the other side of the sheetrock and pulled. A smaller piece came off, but she didn't hit herself in the face, so she counted it as a win.

"Nice," he said, taking the chunk from her. He tossed them in the blue bin and turned around to start marking the other wall.

After a minute, they settled into the work, the silence between them actually really nice. She pounded and ripped, and he cut and stepped.

"Did you grow up here?" he asked.

"I sure did," she said. "My older sister is married and lives on Maui now. My dad left about five years ago and lives on the mainland now. And I have a younger sister on Oahu."

"So you're in Getaway Bay alone."

"I have a cousin on the north side," she said. "And my mother still lives here. Does real estate around the island, mostly for really rich people up on the bluff."

"Mm."

"What about you?" she asked.

"I grew up here as well," he said. "I'm the oldest of four boys."

"I'm surprised we didn't know each other growing up," she said, swinging the hammer. "How old are you?"

"Almost forty," he said. "And I know better than to ask a woman how old she is." He wore a smile in his voice, and Lisa giggled.

"Wise man," she said. "But I'm thirty-six. That's not that far apart."

"I was raised up in the jungly part of the island," he said. "My parents still live up there. They help a lot with Sierra."

"Jungly part," she said, fully flirting with him now. "Sounds intriguing."

"Where's your mom?"

"She's just a mile or two away," she said. "Around toward the volcano."

"Okay, sure," he said.

Another bang rang out in the house, startling her again. She turned to find him pounding out sections of the wall too. He definitely worked much faster than her, and with two of them swinging hammers, they didn't talk over the noise.

Before she knew it, all the walls in the hall, living room, and kitchen were cleared of the wet sheetrock.

Her stomach growled and she put the hammer on the table. "I'll make lunch."

"I'll get the bedroom walls cut," he said.

Lisa wasn't the greatest cook on the planet, but she could put together sandwiches and fruit. A dose of self-consciousness hit her, and she worried that maybe Cal didn't like pineapple or mango.

Then she reminded herself they lived on a tropical island, filled with fruit. If he didn't want to eat it, he didn't have to.

"It's ready," she called over her shoulder, and he came down the hall.

"Thanks," he said. "You don't have to make me lunch. I brought something."

"It's fine," she said, pulling out a chair at the table. "You're here, working on my house."

"You're going to pay me," he said, but he sat down and pulled the plate with the turkey sandwich on it toward him.

"Still," she said, joining him at the table. She took a bite of her sandwich and decided to make sure he knew she was interested. At almost forty years old, though, he had to know already.

She reminded herself that he'd been married and had a fourteen-year-old. So he'd probably been married for a long time.

"How long were you married?" she asked.

He coughed and swallowed his bite of sandwich. "Uh, sixteen years."

"Wow," she said. "You must've gotten married quite young."

"She was a year older than me," he said. "I was twenty-one."

Lisa swallowed, trying not to feel like a complete failure. He'd lived a completely different life than hers. A real life, with a wife and family. A company he owned and operated. If they ended up together, it would be as if he had a second life while she was still waiting for hers to begin.

He focused on his phone and sent several texts. "Just checking with my crew," he said.

"It's fine," Lisa said. "But maybe you should send me a text, and then I'll have your number."

He lifted his eyes to hers, and the crackle between them practically had sound in her ears.

"Ready?" she asked, and he swiped and tapped.

"Ready."

Chapter Six

C al's pulse rippled through his body while Lisa gave him her number. He added it to his phone and then sent her a text. His daughter had taught him the finer ways of emojis, and since he was sitting right in front of the woman he was texting, he sent her a simple thumbs up.

She grinned at her phone and turned it over, bringing her attention back to him. His whole body felt heated, and he had no idea what to say. Many years had passed since he'd had to worry about flirting, talking to a woman, or making sure he was what she might want.

He speared another piece of mango and put it in his mouth, and Lisa asked, "When did you start your construction firm?"

"Oh, let's see," Cal said, trying to get his brain to work through the hormones. He had no idea someone his age could even feel this way, because he hadn't even thought about dating since Jo's death. "Maybe a year or two after Jo and I got married? We hadn't had Sierra yet, so fifteen years ago." With every word he said, he settled a little bit more.

"Wow," she said, taking another bite of her sandwich. "You like it?"

"Love it," he said. "I always knew I'd have a job with my hands. My dad was a boat maker. Well, he still is, when he can drag himself out to the shop." Cal chuckled. "He'd rather go fishing these days, than build the boat to do it."

"I'll bet," Lisa said. "I'm tired of dragging myself to work too." Something sharp entered her eyes, and she stilled, her fork in mid-air. "I mean…."

"It's okay to not like your job," he said.

"I like my job," she said with a sigh.

"Doesn't sound like it," he said gently, watching her. She was so beautiful—and so different from Jo, from her hair color to her perky personality.

"I do," she said. "We've just had a lot of changes at Your Tidal Forever, and I'm still adjusting."

Cal nodded and finished his lunch. "All right, Miss Lisa. We've got a ton more to do today to get your house ready to be put back together again. You ready?"

She stuffed the last bite of her sandwich in her mouth and nodded. He helped her clean up the dishes, and then they got back to work. He couldn't help looking at her every few minutes. No matter what he asked her to do, she did it, and he admired that.

They chatted about their families and pets, and she said, "Next time you come, you'll have to bring Luna. Suzy would love a new dog pal."

"I haven't been letting her out," Cal said. "I don't want her to step on something around the island."

"Smart," Lisa said. "But my house will be put back together soon enough, and then you can bring her."

Cal thought of his German shepherd-golden retriever mix, and yes, Luna would love to romp around with the little French bulldog Lisa owned. He hadn't seen Suzy get off the couch once while he'd been working, and Luna liked a nap on the sofa as much as the next dog.

"All right," he said, straightening to stretch his back. A groan came out of his mouth before he could silence it, and instant humiliation moved through him. He sounded like his seventy-four-year-old father, with aching bones.

"You okay?" Lisa asked, standing too and arching her own back. "I feel like I've been hit by a truck." She moved into the kitchen and pulled down a bottle of pills. "You want some?"

"Yes," he said, joining her in the kitchen. He took the medicine she gave him and waited for her to fill a glass with water, which she handed to him. Her blue eyes burned into him as he swallowed the pills, and the moment between them felt like someone had enveloped them in a magnetic field.

"Lisa?" he asked, his voice so low it wouldn't have been heard outside of the bubble of electricity pulsing around the two of them. "Would you go to dinner with me?"

A smile burst across her face, enhancing her beauty. "Why do you think I gave you my number?" She giggled and stepped into his arms.

Cal had no idea how to hold a woman anymore, but he managed to embrace her. Drawing in a deep, deep breath, he realized how wonderful this human connection felt.

"I'd love to go to dinner with you," Lisa whispered.

"Great," Cal said, his voice hardly his own. "I'll see what's open and operating and let you know."

She stepped back, and Cal waited for the awkwardness to descend on them. But it didn't. She turned back to the sink and started loading the dishwasher with their lunch dishes, and Cal turned to survey the house.

"I'll check the moisture levels again," he said. "And get the fans set up. And you'll be good for a few days."

"And then?" she asked.

"And then I'll come back with my crew and rebuild any studs that need replacing. We'll put up new drywall and texture it. We'll fix any soft wood in the flooring and put down new stuff." He toed the subfloor where they stood. "I don't think your floor is going to need much. Do you want the same thing you had?"

"Sure," she said. "Do I order that, or will you?"

"We'll do it all, through your HOA," he said with a smile. "I better get things finished here and check in with my guys." He looked at her, the connection between them strong when their eyes met. "It was good to see you, Lisa."

She tucked a loose wisp of hair and ducked her head. "Good to see you, too, Cal."

He finished at her house quickly and met up with Adam, Cody, Dave, and Marcos to find out how things had gone in the other houses. Because they'd done considerably less flirting with the homeowners assigned to them, his crew had managed to get the six houses on their list demo'ed and drying.

"So far, so good," Cal said, looking around at his employees. Friends. "We'll meet here tomorrow and do the same thing again."

"Are we matching paint?" Adam asked.

"I need to talk to Hailey," Cal said. "My homeowner asked about flooring."

"Also a concern," Cody confirmed. "We should get things ordered if we want to get this community done on time."

"I'll stop by the office now," Cal said, though his feet hurt and his stomach grumbled for food. He hadn't eaten the lunch he'd brought, and Sierra would hopefully have dinner ready when he got home.

The crew broke up, and Cal lifted his phone to his ear to call his daughter. "Hey, nugget," he said. "Dinner?"

"I just put a half a chicken in the pressure cooker," she said. "And I'm making pasta right now."

Relief filled Cal. And love. "Thank you, bug. I have

to stop by the HOA office before I'm headed home, but I should be there soon."

"All right," Sierra said, and Cal heard himself in his daughter's voice.

He met with Hailey, and they made a plan for supplies. She'd be emailing all the residents to let them know they had one paint choice provided through the HOA, or they could provide their own, and Cal's crew would paint the repaired part of the walls. The HOA would be providing two types of flooring—carpet or a hard laminate. Again, residents could provide their own flooring and his crew would get it installed.

"I need to know soon," he said. "By Monday. Then I can put in the orders and have the supplies when we're ready for them."

"I'll tell them to fill out the survey by then," she said, and Cal nodded.

"Thanks." He rose and went out to his truck, wishing everyone he worked with was as professional. The specs he got from Your Tidal Forever were always exact, and he did enjoy working with them.

His other long-term contact was with the Getaway Bay Theater Company, and their stage pieces were a bit more fluid. And dealing with blueprints and plans through a contractor seemed to change on a daily basis. New home construction was one of Cal's least favorite contracts with his company, but they paid well.

He just didn't like the fact that his beloved Getaway

Bay was getting bigger, as he much preferred trees for neighbors.

He sighed as he pulled into his driveway, which was lined with trees on one side, separating him and Sierra from the neighbors. Jolene had loved that part of the house, because she'd been a shy, private person. A self-proclaimed hermit.

Cal smiled thinking about his late wife. "I met someone new, Jo," he said. "And I know it took three years, but I did it."

His wife had been sick for twenty-five months before she'd passed away. She'd planned her own funeral and said all of her good-byes to the people she loved. They'd all been there, surrounding her bed, when she'd died.

Cal still slept in that bed, still raised their daughter in the house they'd bought and fixed up together, still loved his wife deeply.

But she'd wanted him to move on after she died. She'd made him promise to get out there and "meet someone new, Cal. Mingle."

Mingle.

As if Cal knew how to do that.

A smile touched his mouth, and he got out of the truck. Inside the house, the scent of Alfredo sauce almost covered the smell of fresh paint, and his stomach reminded him of how hungry it was.

In the kitchen, Sierra had her music playing through the speaker on top of the fridge. He reached up to turn the volume down and said, "Hey. How did things go at the school?"

"Good," she said. "We're starting again on Monday." She flashed him a smile that seemed a little strained around the edges.

"That's good," he said. "Only a few more weeks until summer anyway."

"Dad, there's eight weeks until summer break." She rolled her eyes, because she was constantly teasing Cal that he had no sense of time. And he didn't, so he never argued back with her. "And now we have to go for an extra week."

"Yeah, that's a bummer," he said, though he didn't think having his daughter tied up at school was a bad thing. Otherwise, she really had nothing to do. And a teenager with nothing to do could easily find themselves in trouble.

"Dinner's almost ready," she said. "I'm just getting this sauce a little thicker."

"I'll go shower," Cal said, and he left her in the kitchen.

Ten minutes later, freshly washed and with damp hair, Cal sat at the bar with his daughter. "I wanted to talk to you about something," he said, the words clogging his throat.

"If it's about Travis—" she started.

"It's not," he said, because they'd already had that argument. Sierra had promised to tell Cal everything, and he got free access to her phone. If she found herself in trouble with the boy, he'd made her promise to call him, anytime. Day or night. He couldn't help worrying about his daughter, and he'd often felt like he was fumbling in the dark for the past three years as she moved from child to teenager.

"It's about me," he said. "And my, uh, dating life."

"Dating life?" Sierra burst out laughing. "Dad, never say that again." She shook her head as she continued to chuckle.

"What would you prefer?" he asked, glad the mood was light between them. "Love life?"

"Ew, no." She looked at him, and Cal could see so much of Jo in her. "Who are you going out with?"

"Lisa Ashford," he said. "The blonde woman that was with me on the day of the tsunami?" He watched Sierra for her reaction. If she had one, she didn't show it.

"She seemed nice," his daughter said, and Cal nodded.

"I just asked her to dinner," he said. "We haven't gone yet or anything."

A few seconds of silence passed, and then Sierra asked. "So how's this going to work? You want me to meet her? You want to go out with her a few times first?"

Cal had no idea how to date as a single parent. He didn't know he needed rules for himself. Or a plan for Sierra.

He thought through what he wanted, and Sierra let him have the time he needed. "I think I'd like to go out with her a few times first," he said slowly. "See how things are going between us. I think she could meet you once I feel good about it." He looked at Sierra. "Sound good?"

"Yeah," she said.

"You know you're the most important person in my life, right?" he asked, needing her to know this.

She rolled her eyes. "I know, Dad."

"Seriously, Sea," he said, putting his hand on her arm. "I don't—I haven't—I love your mother."

Sierra sobered and simply looked at him. "I know that, Dad. I also know she wanted you to move on and meet someone new."

"She did." Didn't mean a new relationship would be easy. "She can't be replaced."

"No." Sierra shook her head, her dark hair swinging with the motion. "She can't."

Cal slid his arm around his daughter. "I miss her, too."

Sierra leaned her head against Cal's chest and they just breathed together. Then she said, "And if you need help with your date, let me know."

"Do I need help?" he asked.

Sierra straightened and he dropped his arm. She surveyed him, and Cal didn't like the calculating glint in her eye. "No jeans with paint stains on them," she said. "And you need a haircut."

"Well, get out the scissors, nugget," he said. He rolled his eyes. "I am who I am. And she's seen me with this hair."

"But when you go out with her, you want to look *better*," Sierra said. "Then she'll know you made an effort —for her."

"Is that what she wants?" Cal asked, because he honestly had no idea.

"Yes, Dad," his daughter said. "That's what she wants." She smiled and shook her head. "If you need any dating advice, just come see me."

Horror struck Cal right behind his lungs. Dating advice. From his fourteen-year-old daughter. "I don't even want to know what you know," he said, and he wasn't kidding though Sierra burst out laughing.

He was just going to be himself, and if that wasn't good enough for Lisa Ashford…. Well, then they weren't meant to be.

But he supposed he could get a haircut and at least look like he'd made an effort to look nice for her.

Chapter Seven

Lisa honestly could get used to staying at the Sweet Breeze Resort. Everything from the décor to the people who worked there made her feel comfortable, and she'd been able to ignore her nerves over this first real date with Cal—until now.

Until he'd texted that he was just parking and would be up to the eleventh floor soon. She'd offered to meet him in the lobby, but there wasn't much of one of those. The third floor then, she'd said.

But he'd refused, saying a gentleman always came to the door to pick up his date.

Lisa stood in front of the mirror in the hotel bathroom, double-checking her earrings, then her lip gloss, then her shoes.

She loved heels, but Cal had seen her with blood dripping from her foot just a couple of days ago. She didn't need to impress him with her footwear. Nor could she really wear heels at the moment, because of that nasty nail she'd stepped on.

The island of Getaway Bay seemed to be getting itself back together. Lisa could've stayed at Riley's house, which was up high enough to have avoided any water damage. But the house was somewhat remote, and Lisa felt like being around people on the island.

She loved watching the news at night, something delectable from one of the operational restaurants on a tray in front of her, as they chronicled the groups that had come together to help each other get back on their feet. Churches, schools, businesses, and friends had banded together to make sure everyone had help.

Her mother's neighbors had taken her in, and Lisa thought about texting her, just to tell her about Cal. Just as quickly as that thought had come, Lisa dismissed it. Her mother had turned into a bit of a male-hater since her husband had left her after almost forty years of marriage.

Lisa couldn't really blame her, but that didn't mean she wanted to listen to her mother's lecture about the demerits all men possessed. She had some hope left for herself, and her heart shot out an extra beat.

"Where is he?" she murmured to Suzy, who raised her head off the pillow on the bed. The dog said nothing and flopped back down, already asleep again. Lisa reminded herself that the hotel was operating on half the number of elevators since the tsunami. They had a narrow walkway roped off on the first floor that led from the bank of elevators to the parking garage while they worked on repairs, and there could very well be a line to get upstairs.

She wandered over to the window and gazed down on the beach below. The sand was crowded, and it seemed like there was no evidence of the tsunami's force at all. Of course, Fisher DuPont, owner of Sweet Breeze, had probably made sure the beach clean-up was top priority. Lisa would've done the same thing, had she owned this place. In fact, Hope had started working with a private company like Cal's to clean up the beaches they regularly used for their weddings.

A few minutes later, a loud knock made her gasp and spin toward the door. Suzy barked, and Lisa shushed her. "It's Cal, silly."

She strode across the room and whipped open the door to find Cal standing there, his brown hair sculpted just-so. She had the sudden urge to run her fingers along his jawline, just to feel the full beard he wore there. The hair on his face was a couple of shades darker than on his head, and it was oh-so-sexy.

"Hey," he said, clearly out of breath. "Sorry I'm a bit late."

"You're fine." She honestly had no idea what time it even was. Or where he was taking her.

"The line for the elevators was really long." He reached for her hand. "Are you ready? Need a purse or anything?"

Lisa held up one finger and dashed back to the

cabinet that housed the TV. She picked up her card holder and put it in her pocket, glad she'd chosen to wear this black jumpsuit, precisely because it did have pockets.

"Ready," she said, moving back toward him. He'd come into the room a little bit, his right foot holding the spring-loaded door open.

"You're…beautiful," he said, his eyes scanning her body and rebounding back to her face. "Simply stunning."

"Stunning?" She grinned at him, pure satisfaction moving through her. She had worked hard on her makeup, contouring her face just right. Her silver earrings dripped into teardrop shapes, and she'd even gone for a manicure today. And any day spent at the salon was a good day.

"I haven't had anyone call me stunning in a while," she said, tripping her fingertips up the front of his shirt to his collar. "Or maybe ever." Her eyes met his, and it seemed like a moment where a man might kiss her.

But Cal didn't, and Lisa realized in that single breath of time that he was unlike any other man she'd ever dated before. Because any of them would've kissed her then.

And Cal didn't.

At the same time, she knew it wasn't because he didn't want to. It was because he respected her more than any other man she'd been out with.

"It's true," he said, his voice hoarse.

"Well, I love this shirt," she said, focusing on the navy blue button-up. "What are those?"

"Sierra told me I had to wear it," he said, sliding one arm around Lisa's waist. Oh, she liked the way he'd claimed her, the way tingling sparks shot up her spine. "They're actually sailboats." He looked down at his shirt too. "I feel ridiculous."

He started laughing, and that made happiness explode through Lisa. She joined him, tucking her hand into his and stepping with him as they moved into the hall. "What would you normally wear?" she asked. "If you didn't have your daughter dressing you."

"I don't know," he said. "Probably just a T-shirt. Something comfortable."

"That shirt isn't comfortable?" Because it looked like it had been tailored just for him.

"It's fine," he said. "I probably should've asked you where you wanted to eat. I thought Indian House might be good."

"Oh, I love Indian House," she said. "And we did the wedding for Zara, the woman who married the prince?"

"Oh," Cal said, and he clearly didn't keep up with the social happenings on the island.

"Her family owns Indian House," Lisa said to clarify. "They have delicious food."

"It's one of my favorite places on the whole island." Cal grinned at her. "Want to brave waiting for the elevator? Or should we take the stairs?"

She couldn't believe he'd climbed eleven flights of

stairs just to see her, and warmth filled her body. "Let's be brave," she said, reaching to push the down button.

"How's the house drying?" he asked.

"I don't know," she said. "I don't have one of those fancy moisture things." Flirting with him was fun and came naturally to her.

He chuckled. "I'll come see on Monday. We'll have demo done on the rest of the houses tomorrow, and then the rebuilding begins."

"How long until I'm out of here?" she asked, surprised when the elevator dinged and the white light on the wall lit up. "And look. We only had to wait a few seconds."

"A miracle," he said, gazing at her with a heated edge in those dark blue eyes. They stepped onto the elevator, and he said, "You should be able to move back into your place by the end of the week. I don't think it'll take that long to get the supplies and get them in. In fact, once we get the flooring, it'll only take a day to get it laid."

"Perfect," she said. Sweet Breeze had offered deep discounts or completely free rooms for those displaced by the tsunami, and Lisa did like the room service. But Suzy hated being cooped up in the hotel room, and Lisa could admit that she did too. Both of them much preferred the small lawn that had palm trees bordering the fence in the back.

"I've almost got my yard cleaned up," she said.

"That's great," he said. "I haven't had time to come

help." He cut a glance at her, and Lisa smiled at him and grabbed onto his hand with both of hers.

"It's okay, Cal. I can rake and pick up branches and fronds."

"I know you can. I've seen you with a hammer." He grinned at her, and Lisa felt like the luckiest woman in the world. How had she overlooked this gem of a man for so long?

"Will there be dancing tonight?" she asked.

"Not at Indian House," he said, stepping off the elevator and taking her with him. They squeezed past the long line of people waiting to go up, walking between a sheet of plastic on one side and a set of ropes to contain a crowd on the other.

Heat hit her as she walked into the parking garage, and Cal handed his ticket to Sterling. The valet glanced at it and then Lisa, and said, "Coming up, sir."

Cal drove a big, rumbly truck, and Lisa felt like a celebrity as he helped her up onto the seat. Wearing this jumpsuit always made her feel like she stood out, though, and she gathered her hair together and combed her fingers through the curls as Cal rounded the front of the truck.

"What's your favorite food?" she asked as he started the drive to Indian House.

"Ever? Out of anything?"

"Yes, that's what a favorite is," she teased.

He glanced at her again, a nervous energy pouring off of him now. "My wife used to make the most amazing key lime pie," he said. "I'd eat that for every meal if I could."

"Mm, key lime pie," Lisa said, though her mouth puckered as if she'd taken a bite of the sour dessert right then. But Cal had been married before—for a long time —and she couldn't expect him to never mention his wife.

"How did Jo die?" she asked next.

Cal cleared his throat. "Uterine cancer. We were very lucky to get Sierra at all."

"I'm so sorry," Lisa said.

"We knew for a long time before she died," Cal said. "And we got many more months with her than they said we would."

"Still sucks."

Cal gave a burst of a laugh. "Yes, it does." He turned and started up toward the restaurant. "What about you, Lisa? Serious relationships I should know about?"

"Oh, no," she said in mock seriousness. "I've dated a lot of men, but I wouldn't say any of them were very serious."

"No serious relationships?" he asked, as if he didn't believe her.

"I mean, I dated a guy for eight months once. I think that was the longest relationship I've had. I guess it was serious."

"You guess?"

"Well, I never got a diamond," she said. "We sort of just...hung out." She thought of Chuck. Yes, she'd liked the guy. She'd kissed him. "He was more of an outdoor enthusiast than I was willing to commit to."

Cal burst out laughing again, but Lisa wasn't quite sure what was so funny. "You must like doing things outside," she said.

"I mean, I guess."

"You guess?" she repeated, much the same as him. They laughed together, and Lisa's heart sang.

"Chuck was into parasailing. Sea kayaking. Rock climbing." She shook her head. "He was an extreme tour guide, and I kind of like to lay by the pool."

"Yeah, an online calendar type of woman," he said with a grin.

"Yes," she said. "You so get me."

He pulled into Indian House and found a spot to park at the back of the lot. "So I love coffee, and you love laying by the pool."

"And we both love Indian food," she said. "Sounds like a match made in heaven, doesn't it?" She laughed so he'd know she wasn't really serious, but her mind rotated around the idea of having her first serious relationship with Cal during the rest of their dinner.

He walked her all the way back to the eleventh floor and handed her the leftover butter chicken. "I had a great time tonight," he said, leaning one hand against the doorframe. Lisa hadn't even taken out her electronic key yet. "What do you think about going out with me again?"

Lisa looked up at him, and his soul was so kind and so big. She wanted to spend a lot more time with him, so she tipped up onto her toes and touched her lips to his cheek, barley pulling away to say, "I'd love to go out with you again."

Their body heat mingled, and Lisa stayed on her toes for another moment before settling and turning to open her door. "You just tell me when you're available. I have to go back to work on Monday, but I don't do a whole lot in the evenings."

"Me either," he said, his voice trapped down deep in his chest.

Lisa smiled at him over her shoulder, unlocked her door, and went into her room. "Good-night, Cal."

"Night." He didn't look away from her as she carefully let the door come closed between them. A sigh filled her whole body, and she let it out as she waltzed into the room and picked up her pup.

"He's *wonderful*," she told Suzy. "And I just know you're going to love him, and his dog, and his daughter." She danced with the French bulldog for a moment, putting the dog down when she squirmed.

Lisa stood at the window, the beach in the dark just as spectacular as the day. Everything seemed so twinkly, including every nerve ending in her body. Her mind raced, but she pulled back on the accelerator, reminding herself not to get too far ahead of reality.

After all, every first date she'd been on had felt this magical—and sometimes she couldn't even get the guy to call her for a second.

"But Cal's already asked," she whispered to herself,

and she closed her eyes in a long blink while giddiness galloped through her.

Still, she told herself. *Don't fall too fast.*

Lisa silenced the voice as she got ready for bed. Because if she knew how to fall slowly, she'd have done that in the past and saved herself all the broken hearts.

Chapter Eight

C al checked Lisa's house while she was at work, and her house didn't have the same spirit it possessed while she was inside it. Suzy didn't seem too terribly worried to find him there, and he wondered if she made the drive from the hotel to her house to drop off the dog every day.

Probably. Lisa was a creature of habit—he'd learned that over the last few days as they'd stayed in contact.

Sierra had assured him that "at least half" of dating now was done through a device, and the yawn pulling through his whole body testified of that. His late-night texting sessions with Lisa had kept him awake much later than normal.

Her walls had been dry when he'd gone by on Monday, and he'd marked his map with a green star so the crew would know the repairs were ready to be completed. The supplies had been ordered. The hours slipped away, each one full and busy, just the way Cal liked them. That way, he didn't have a lot of mental room for his thoughts to take over. When he realized he'd been thinking more about Lisa than Jo for the past week, he paused, trying to figure out how he felt about that.

His phone buzzed, and Cal pulled it from his pocket, hoping Lisa had texted him the answer to where she'd like to go to dinner that night. He'd worked too much to see her during the week, but it was Friday, and he wanted another weekend date with the stunning blonde woman. Maybe she'd wear another fancy pantsuit that left her shoulders bare except for a couple of thin straps. Or that intoxicating perfume he couldn't seem to get out of his nose.

But the message was from his daughter. *Can I go to the outdoor cinema tonight?*

"This goes on the entire first floor?" Adam asked, and Cal looked up from his phone.

"Yep," he said, pocketing his device so he could help Adam bring in the boxes of flooring that were going down in Lisa's house that day. He didn't want to tell his daughter no, but he didn't want to give his permission for her to go out with Travis either. The outdoor cinema served dinner along with a show, and he didn't even know what was playing.

His phone buzzed again, and he was sure that was Sierra, telling him what the menu was and what they'd be watching. He had no real reason for why he didn't want her to go, and he'd be out himself that night.

He certainly didn't want Sierra to be home alone tonight. If she invited Travis over while he wasn't there....

He yanked his phone from his back pocket and saw the menu and the movie. *Sure,* he typed out, glad for texting in moments like these. Then he didn't have to worry that his voice had sounded too fake or too growly or whatever.

Thanks, Dad, Sierra said, sending a smiley face too. *You're going out with Lisa again, right?*

Right.

Have fun! I'll check in with you when I get home.

Cal sighed and looked up again. Before he could even take one step to go help his crew, his phone rang. Lisa's name sat on the screen, and he ducked out of her house and walked along the porch toward the corner as he answered it.

"Hey," she said brightly. "I just got your text. I was thinking...there's a great movie playing at the outdoor cinema tonight. They have food, and drinks, and the show...." She let her voice hang there, and Cal almost started laughing.

"I know about the outdoor cinema," he said. "I think they're serving coconut shrimp tonight."

"Always," she said.

"And you want to do that?"

"Sometimes they have dancing," she said, which was code for yes, she wanted to go to the outdoor cinema.

He should probably tell her his daughter had a date

there that night too, but he didn't. "Sounds great," he said. He could keep an eye on Sierra and Travis from a distance. The outdoor cinema was a big place, and families, couples, and singles came. She would never know he'd been there—unless she asked, of course.

She hadn't questioned him about his date with Lisa last weekend, so he had no reason to think she would this time.

"Pick me up at six?" Lisa asked.

"Actually, I'll probably still be at your house at six," he said, pressing his back into the house behind him. He heard someone climbing the steps, huffing and puffing under the weight of the flooring, and guilt moved through him. "We're here now, getting the floor done."

"And then the house is done, right?"

"That's right. I told you the end of the week. You can move back home tomorrow."

"You're the best, Cal. I have to run, but I'll see you tonight."

"Yeah," he said. "See you." The call ended, and he really should go help his guys get the flooring in. But he stayed against the wall, the privacy it gave him necessary for another few moments.

He couldn't believe how much he liked this woman, as she was nothing like Jo. "It's okay, right?" he whispered, somehow asking his late wife to put her stamp of approval on this relationship.

A sense of calmness came over him, and when Cody asked, "Where did Cal go?" he stepped around the corner and said, "I'm right here. Sorry, phone call." He joined his crew, who had brought in all the boxes they needed for Lisa's house, and together, the five of them got started with laying her new floor.

——————

CAL WAS NOT AT LISA'S AT SIX. HE'D LEFT ADAM AND Cody to finish the last hundred square feet of flooring so he could race home to be there when Sierra went out. He trusted his daughter, but he wanted her to know he was paying attention.

So when she came out of her room wearing a flimsy tank top that showed her bra on the sides and the full back, he straightened from the counter where he'd been leaning. "Yeah, you need to wear something else," he said.

"Dad," she said.

"Nope," he said. "Turn around."

She sighed in an exaggerated way, but she did what he asked. "I can see your entire back," he said. "And that bra is all lace. It looks like you're wearing lingerie." He hated seeing her undergarments. They were supposed to be *under* the clothes, not showing through.

Sierra faced him again, and Cal felt a flash of love for her. "Honey," he said. "I know it's not your job to make sure boys don't think bad thoughts. But you *can* consider their feelings. Travis sees you wearing that, and I guarantee he's going to be thinking about getting that bra all the way off."

"Ew, Dad, can we not talk about this?"

"Sure," he said. "Go put on a different shirt, and we won't have to talk about it."

She stared at him, clearly trying to decide if she should push this or not. Cal looked steadily back at her, so glad he'd come home instead of staying to finish Lisa's floor. Yes, he wanted to see her, but there was time to be a father *and* a boyfriend.

Boyfriend.

Yikes, he hadn't been one of those in a while.

"Fine," Sierra said, turning and walking back to her room. She could've stomped, and she didn't, so Call called, "Thank you, bug," after her.

Her bedroom door closed a little too hard, but Cal honestly didn't care. "Wish you were here to deal with the wardrobe thing, Jo," he whispered to the window overlooking the backyard. In fact, there were a lot of things he'd handled that he'd wished his wife had been there for. But he and Sierra had survived their first bra-buying trip, and the first time he'd had to purchase feminine hygiene products for her.

Thankfully, his mother had helped out with both of those things too, and Cal wasn't completely left to his own devices.

Sierra returned, wearing a light purple tank top with thick shoulder straps that hid her bra. The fabric went up much higher under her arms, and her entire back was covered.

"Beautiful," Cal said, stepping over to her and embracing her. "You know you're beautiful, right?"

"I guess," she said, holding onto him.

"You are," he said, leaning back and tucking her hair behind her ear. "With the makeup, or without it. And definitely more beautiful when it's a little bit of a mystery what your skin looks like." He grinned at her. "Now go have fun. Be safe. Call me if anything happens."

"I will, Dad."

"Love you."

"Love you, too." Sierra gave him a smile and walked out the front door.

He sighed and looked down at Luna. "She's okay, right?"

Luna cocked her head as if she could understand Cal's question and really wanted to answer it.

"She is," he said. "Let's get you fed, and then I have to go again." He rinsed out the dog's bowl and refilled it with fresh water. He scooped new food into another bowl and set it by the back door. "I'll take you to the park tomorrow," he promised. "I'm not working."

He'd been going, going, going for twelve days straight now. He needed a day off, and in fact, he was taking the whole weekend away from the Avenues.

And he was also late to pick up Lisa. He hurried down the hall to change his clothes, his phone at his ear.

"Hey," he said. "I had a daughter thing. I'm just leaving my place."

"No problem," she said. "The floor is amazing."

"Yeah?" he asked, stripping off his work shirt. "You like it?"

"I love it."

"Great," he said. "I'll see you soon." Their call ended, and Cal took a few minutes to brush his teeth, wash his hands, and re-comb his hair. With one final look in the mirror, he grabbed a T-shirt from his closet and pulled it over his head on the way down the hall.

The drive to Lisa's only took ten minutes, and she waited for him on her front porch. Plenty of skin was visible along her shoulders, and Cal wasn't even a hormonal, sixteen-year-old boy, but his thoughts danced along the edge of reason.

He wanted to touch that skin. Kiss it. Run his hands along it and down her back.

Lisa stood up, and today, she had her blonde hair pulled up into a high ponytail on top of her head, revealing that slender neck. She wore a denim dress, with thin straps over her shoulders holding it up. The dress fell in loose waves down her body to her feet, where she wore a pair of white sandals.

In short, she was absolutely gorgeous, and Cal couldn't remember how to breathe. Or apparently, get out of his truck, because Lisa arrived while he was still staring.

"Hey," she said, and he blinked.

"Sorry," he said. "You're just so pretty, and I…." He got out of the truck and took her into his arms. A sigh moved through his body, especially when Lisa hugged him back.

"I see you've got the comfortable T-shirt on this time," she teased, and Cal laughed as he released her.

"I mean, it's the outdoor cinema."

"So I'm overdressed? Is that it?" Her blue eyes glittered at him, and Cal suddenly had thoughts about kissing her.

Kissing her.

Wild.

He hadn't kissed anyone for three years, and before that, he and Jo had been together for so long. Nerves paraded through him. What if he'd forgotten how to kiss a woman?

"You're not overdressed," he said. "You look great." He walked her around to the passenger side and helped her up.

"So, for full disclosure," he said once he was behind the wheel and they were headed toward the outdoor cinema. "My daughter is going to be at the cinema tonight, too."

"Oh, okay. Am I meeting her tonight?" Lisa pressed her lips together, and Cal wondered if that was a show of nerves.

"I don't know," he said. "It's a big place. We might not see her."

"So we'll just see how it goes."

"Right," he said.

"How did that happen? Us going to the same place?"

"She texted literally two minutes before you called and suggested it." He shrugged. "I didn't really think about you meeting her until now." He had wanted to go to the same place as Sierra, and with Lisa at his side, it wouldn't seem like he was following her because he didn't trust her.

He did trust his daughter.

"I'm sure it'll be fine," Lisa said. "I met her briefly after the tsunami, remember?"

"Yeah, but that wasn't a real meeting," Cal said, his nerves firing again.

"How will you introduce me?" Lisa asked.

Cal turned into the parking lot, cursing himself for being late. There were cars everywhere, and he should've known they'd be busy, as the movie theater closer to the ocean was still closed.

"Uh, introduce you?"

"Yeah, am I a friend, a girlfriend, your date…?"

Cal spied a spot and pulled into it. "We'll have to walk a bit."

"Okay," Lisa said, still watching him. "And you'll say, 'Hey, honey, this is Lisa Ashford, my…'?"

"Well, I think it's obvious I want to be more than friends."

"Oh, obviously," Lisa said with a smile.

"And we are on a date."

"True."

"And…." Cal ground his words into silence in his throat and shrugged again. "I don't know. What qualifies a woman as a girlfriend?"

"That's up to you, Cal."

He felt very out of his element. He had no idea what his qualifications for a girlfriend were. Twenty years ago, when he was dating, if he went out with a woman several times, she was his girlfriend. It was easier. Obvious. They didn't even have conversations like this.

"I think I'd say girlfriend," he said.

"Interesting," Lisa said, unbuckling. "We better get going, or we'll have to buy a seat with the obstructed view."

"Yeah." Cal got out of the truck too and met her at the hood. "What's interesting about me calling you my girlfriend?" he asked.

"I don't know," she said.

"Of course you do." He watched her as he took her hand in his and they started toward the huge building where they'd buy tickets to eat and watch a movie. Lisa didn't say anything, and Cal's insides twisted. Maybe he shouldn't have brought up the G-word. Sometimes he felt like he and Lisa were from two different worlds, though they were close in age.

Chapter Nine

L isa wrestled with her thoughts, trying to get them to play nice inside her head. "I don't usually consider myself someone's girlfriend until we've kissed," she finally said.

"Oh, I see." Cal nodded, his eyes trained on the ground as they walked through the parking lot. "I'm... not ready to do that."

"I know," Lisa said, squeezing his hand. "It's our second date, Cal. I'm not ready for that either."

"So maybe you're not my girlfriend."

"I don't mind," she said. "I'm fine with the label." And she was. In fact, such a label excited her—when it came to Cal. He wasn't the type of man to date four girls a week and call each of them "baby" the way one of her "boyfriends" had.

If he wanted to call her his girlfriend, she really was fine with that.

He stepped up to the ticket booth and started talking to the woman in the window. A few minutes later, they had tickets—with a clear view—and entered the amphitheater. The space spread before her, and Lisa took a deep breath and sighed as she smiled.

"I love this place," she said. She really felt like she'd entered a new city—a hidden gem in the tropical rain forest. The amphitheater had rows and rows of semicircles leading down to a stage. She'd never been here for a live play, but a huge, curved screen rose from there. The movie would be shown there, and she'd watched from her table before, as well as from a seat in the amphitheater itself.

The rows were grass, but they also had chairs, so when it rained, they could still show movies without people sitting on the wet ground. She'd been here when it was raining, and a huge cover had been raised to protect the entire area in front of her.

The atmosphere buzzed with energy as people chatted and laughed, moved between tables, and enjoyed themselves. The top of the amphitheater was open, with dozens and dozens of tables, some for big groups, some for only two.

"We're table ninety-one," Cal said, looking around. "I have no idea where that is."

"We'll find it," Lisa said, linking her arm through his. "Are we sharing?"

"No, table for two."

"Mm, romantic," Lisa said, pressing into his side. "Did you order the buffet or the menu dinner?"

"Menu," he said. "I'm sorry. I should've asked you what you wanted."

"I would've chosen menu." She smiled at him, and added, "That's forty-seven. Let's go back this way." She led him to the right, stepping around a waiter and a busboy, several other people, and entering the maze of tables.

"Eighty-five is over there," Cal said, and Lisa took another right." A minute later, they found table ninety-one, a cozy little table with a pineapple in the middle for decoration. Lisa took in a breath of the perfumed air, as tropical fruit trees, palms, and banyans made up two sides of the outdoor cinema. And the building where they'd bought their tickets made up the fourth side, creating an intimate space though it was so large.

"Did you see your daughter?" Lisa asked, because Cal was obviously searching for her.

His attention came back to her. "No, I didn't. Let's sit." He pulled out her chair for her, and Lisa sat. Not a moment later, a waiter appeared and picked up the receipt Cal had put on the table.

"I'm Jonathan, and I'll be taking care of you tonight. Menus," he said, pulling them out of the front pocket of his apron. "Drinks for you tonight?"

Cal looked at Lisa, and she smiled up at the waiter. "Mango lemonade."

"Water for me," Cal said.

"Do you not drink soda?" she asked as Jonathan left.

"Not usually," he said. "A few years ago, I had four kidney stones from all the cola I drank." He gave half a shrug. "I gave it up then."

"Flavored lemonades are my kryptonite." She laid her arms on the table and leaned into them. "What's yours, Cal Lewiston?" She cocked her head, trying to see more of this man.

He chuckled and shook his head. "I don't know if I should tell you. I feel like you're going to use it against me."

She glanced up as the waiter set her pale orange lemonade on the table. "Definitely," she said, stirring the straw around in the glass.

"Do you guys need a few more minutes?" Jonathan asked. "We take kitchen orders until an hour before the end of the film. Tonight, that's at eight-fifty."

"We need a minute," Cal said, opening his menu for the first time.

"I'll circle back," Jonathan said.

Lisa looked at her menu too, but she already knew what she wanted. She pretended to look for the salmon pinwheel with wild rice she loved, but she really just watched Cal search the tables in his view.

Something was going on with his daughter, and Lisa wondered if she should suggest they just go find her. Her stomach clenched, because she hadn't prepared herself to formally meet his daughter tonight.

The waiter returned, and Lisa beamed up at him,

closing her menu. "I'll have the king salmon pinwheel, please."

"Just came in an hour ago." He smiled back at her, and he seemed more like the type of man Lisa would go out with. Had she come to the outdoor cinema with her girlfriends, she'd try to get Jonathan's number before the movie started.

Tonight, though, she wasn't even sure what she'd ever seen in a man like Jonathan.

"I'll have the sirloin," Cal said, handing the menu over. "Medium-rare."

"Baked potato or mashed?"

"Mashed," he said. "White gravy, please."

"Be right back." Jonathan left again, and Lisa focused on Cal.

"Steak?" she guessed. "Is that the kryptonite?"

"I already told you coffee was my love language."

"Really? It's coffee?" For some reason, that disappointed her.

"Well, Hawaii has some of the best coffee in the world," he said. "You know we have huge coffee bean farms here, right?"

"Not on this island," she said.

"Yes," he said. "There's one on this island."

"No, they shut it down."

"No, someone else just bought it."

Lisa didn't keep up with all the coffee dealings on the island of Getaway Bay, so she conceded the point. "So if you love coffee so much, why didn't you order it tonight?"

"It's after six," he said. "I don't drink coffee after six, or else I can't sleep."

"I think I'm caffeine immune," Lisa said with a smile.

"Now, if you really want to know what gets me excited, you'll put a scoop of pure vanilla bean ice cream in my coffee." He smacked his lips and grinned like a little boy on his birthday. "That's my kryptonite."

"Coffee float," Lisa said, surprised. "I've never had one of those."

"I'll get some of our local coffee and make you one." Sparks flew from his eyes, and Lisa liked the electricity between them.

She giggled and ducked her head, forgetting that she'd tied her hair up tonight, and it didn't fall down to hide her face the way she wished it would. Her trademark move was to tuck her hair and look up at a man through her eyelashes.

"I'll be right back," Cal said, his voice hard as granite.

"What?" Lisa watched him jump to his feet and stride away. She watched him go, where he stopped several tables over.

His voice was loud, but the din in the large area kept his words from making sense in her ears. She got up and went after him, because he seemed upset—and so did the teenage girl he was talking to.

She arrived at the same time Cal asked, "And who is this? Where's Travis?"

"Dad," Sierra said, her face bright red. "I didn't come with Travis."

"You asked if you could go to the outdoor cinema," he said, glancing at Lisa.

"But I never said I was coming with Travis." She glanced at Lisa, who tried to flash her a smile before she looked away. But the teen seemed to look right through her, and wow, that stung.

"You should've told me if you were coming with a boy I don't know." Cal glared at the boy in question. "How old are you?"

"You don't have to answer that, Justin," Sierra said.

"Someone better answer it," Cal growled.

"I'm seventeen, sir," Justin said, and he seemed semi-mature to Lisa. Her heartbeat ping-ponged around in her chest, because she didn't know what to do in this situation. Side with Cal? Calm him down? Walk away and let him deal with this obvious family matter?

"You realize she's fourteen years old?"

Justin looked at Sierra. "I, uh, actually thought she was older than that, sir."

"Justin," Sierra said.

"Maybe he didn't ask," Cal suggested, a slight sarcastic note to his voice. "Did you just let him assume what he wanted to?"

Sierra didn't answer, and she looked at Lisa again.

She sucked in a breath. "Cal," she said. "Maybe we

should talk about this later." She glanced over her shoulder to see Jonathan standing at their table, setting their plates of food down. "Our dinner just arrived."

Cal looked at her, the frustration in his expression plain to see.

"Cal," she said again, slipping her hands around his arm and hugging it. She wasn't sure what else to say. She didn't want to tell him how to parent his daughter.

"I'll take her home right now, sir," Justin said.

"Dad," Sierra said, and Cal looked back at her.

"I don't want her home alone." He looked at Lisa. "Would you mind if they joined us?"

"Dad, I'm not double-dating with you and your girl-friend." She glanced at Lisa. "Sorry. No offense."

Lisa held up her hand as if to say, *I get it.* "I'm Lisa Ashford, by the way."

"Sorry," Cal said. "Lisa, this is Sierra, my fourteen-year-old daughter who *forgot* to mention she'd broken up with her sixteen-year-old boyfriend and had found another one."

Lisa nodded at the girl. "So nice to meet you, Sierra. Your father has said so many good things about you."

Sierra scanned Lisa, and she felt very much like the fourteen-year-old was sizing her up. She said nothing, and the awkwardness doubled.

"How about they sit near us?" Lisa asked Cal. "So you can see them, but they can still talk, and we can still talk…." She turned and waved to Jonathan, who came over. "Is there a table for these two near us?" she asked.

"Let me check with our seating team." He smiled around at everyone and walked away.

"Cal," Lisa said very quietly, tugging on his arm. "Let's go sit down. Our food is getting cold."

He looked at her with a measure of helplessness in his eyes. She'd seen a look like this before, as she worked with a lot of grooms that were completely overwhelmed with the immensity of planning a wedding.

"Come on," she said with a smile. "They'll sit right by us."

"All right," Cal said, giving one more glare to his daughter. Lisa didn't like that his attention would be divided, but she couldn't very well demand he move past this situation right this second.

Jonathan approached. "I can get them at table eighty-six," he said. "It's a few over and one row behind you." He pointed to it, and Lisa looked at Cal.

"That's fine," he said. "Thank you."

Jonathan nodded, and glanced at Sierra and Justin. "Eighty-six. Did you guys have the buffet or the menu dinner?"

"Buffet," Justin said, and Cal growled low in his throat.

"What?" Lisa asked as everyone moved back to their assigned tables.

"She texted me the menu," he said, shaking his head. They got back to their table, and he picked up his plate. "Would you mind switching sides with me? Then I can glare at them and still face you."

Lisa chuckled, but she knew he wasn't kidding. They switched sides, and Cal stared for a long minute at Sierra and Justin. He finally sighed and picked up his fork. "Sorry. When I saw her with a different boy—holding his hand and flirting—I sort of floated out of my head."

"It's fine," Lisa said. "She's your daughter."

"Yeah." Cal looked down at his steak. "This looks great."

Lisa focused on her food too. "Yeah, mine is like a fish cupcake." She loved the orange swirl of the salmon, the lentils and kale it sat on which made up the paper on the cupcake, the baby greens on top. And the sauce surrounding the fish? The best thing Lisa had ever put in her mouth.

"It sure does," Cal said, finally smiling at her. He cut into his steak, and it looked like a perfect medium rare to Lisa. He put the meat in his mouth, and he moaned. "Oh, this is good."

"You don't come here very often, do you?" she asked.

"No," he admitted. "Big crowd. Expensive food. Single." He cut another bite of steak and swiped it through his mashed potatoes and gravy. "Doesn't really add up to a Friday night at the outdoor cinema, you know?"

"Oh, I know." Lisa didn't want to tell him how many dates she'd been on here, so she just flaked off another bite of her fish and lentils, swirled it in the sauce, and put it in her mouth. Cal did a good job of staying focused on

Lisa and the conversation at their own table, and she appreciated that.

The lights dimmed, and the enormous screen lit up behind her, blue lights flashing on Cal's face. "Are they moving?" she asked. "Do you want to go down to the viewing seats?"

"They are moving," Cal said. "But I'd rather stay here." He met her eye and motioned for her to come over to his side of the table. "Come sit by me."

Lisa was more than happy to cuddle into Cal while they watched a movie, and she got up and pulled her chair over to his side. He took her hand, and she leaned against his shoulder, the arms of the chair a little bit in the way.

She didn't mind though, because Cal had finally relaxed. His hand in hers felt warm and strong, and Lisa wasn't even sure what the movie was or what was happening. Because she was holding Cal's hand, and she could only hope there would be some kissing in their future.

She couldn't even imagine what a kiss shared with him would feel like, but her heartbeat was very excited about it.

Chapter Ten

C al got home several minutes after Sierra, who was already barricaded behind her locked bedroom door. "I know you're in here," he said, knocking on her door. "We have to talk."

He heard something behind the door, and a moment later, Sierra opened it. She wore the same tank top, but instead of the shorts she'd had on earlier, she now wore a pair of pajama shorts. "Look, Dad, I'm sorry."

Yeah, sure sounded like she was. Cal didn't say that, though. He shouldn't have been sarcastic at the outdoor cinema either. Jo would've hated that, and Cal had regretted his angry actions and words with his daughter in public.

"I'm sorry too," he said. "I shouldn't have made a scene at the cinema."

Sierra folded her arms. "I suppose I'm grounded."

"Big time," he said. "I don't understand why you couldn't have just told me you broke up with Travis."

Sierra heaved a great big sigh. "I don't know, Dad. I was…embarrassed." She mumbled the last word, and Cal's heart started cracking.

"Honey," he said. "It's just you and me. You have to tell me stuff."

She nodded, her eyes turning a little glassy. "I know." Her voice broke, and Cal gathered her into his arms. "And Justin seemed so nice, too."

"He wasn't nice?"

"He said he didn't know I was so young, and he just went out with me because I was hot." She cried into his shoulder, and Cal wanted to drape her in a bedsheet every time she left the house, starting tomorrow.

"I'm sorry, bug," he said.

Sierra composed herself quickly, and Cal kept his arm around her. "Let's go see what we have in the freezer."

"There's no coffee," she said.

"I wouldn't be able to sleep anyway," he said. "And I finally have a day off tomorrow, and I want to sleep in." He grinned at her, taking her down the hall to the kitchen. "Then Lisa and I are meeting for lunch. If you want to come, you can."

"Yeah, pass," Sierra said dryly.

"Oh, ho," he said. "What? Are we too old for you? We can go to one of your trendy places."

"It's not that." Sierra opened the freezer, reached in, and handed him a carton of ice cream.

"What is it, then?" he asked.

"She's...do you really like her?" Sierra looked at him, and Cal found seriousness on her face.

"Yeah," Cal said. "I really like her."

"She seems a bit...fake."

"Fake?" Cal could use a lot of words to describe Lisa, but fake wasn't one of them. Never had he thought that.

"Yeah, no one has hair that blonde. And all that jewelry? Who dresses like that?"

"Just because you won't even wear a ring your mom left you, doesn't mean that everyone hates jewelry." He made his voice light, so his daughter would know he was teasing.

"And the clothes. I mean, that dress probably cost a thousand dollars."

"Okay," Cal said. He had enough money, and obviously Lisa did too.

"She, I don't know." Sierra opened a drawer and pulled out an ice cream scoop. "She probably goes to the nail salon weekly. She gets manicures and probably those makeup tests to see which color of lip gloss works with her skin tone. She's shallow."

Cal felt like he'd been hit with a bucket of ice water. He didn't know how to answer. *Fake. Shallow.*

He'd never gotten those vibes from her. They'd had meaningful conversations, and the chemistry between them felt off the charts.

ELANA JOHNSON

"I mean, if you like her, it's fine," Sierra said, but it clearly wasn't fine. "But I don't see how I'll have anything in common with her." She handed him the scoop, and Cal busied himself by dishing up their late-night treat.

They sat at the table together, and Cal still had no idea what to say. If he brought a new woman into his life, he brought her into Sierra's life too. He'd want them to get along. No one could replace Jo as Sierra's mother, but Cal couldn't mediate problems between his new wife and his daughter for the rest of his life. That didn't sound fun at all.

"How long am I grounded?" Sierra asked.

"Let's start with two weeks," he said. "And I want your phone plugged in out here during that time."

"I hate that," Sierra complained. "I need it for my alarm clock."

"And I need to know you're not sending pictures of yourself in that lingerie to *seventeen*-year-old boys who think you're hot." He pinned her with a look that said not to test him on this, and wisely, she didn't argue.

"In fact," Cal said. "I'd like to see the phone right now." He held out his hand and took a bite of the peanut butter ice cream. "You didn't erase the texts, did you?"

Sierra heaved a sigh and got up. "No, Dad. I didn't erase the texts."

"Good, because if you had, you wouldn't have a phone until you're eighteen."

"I know, I know." Sierra semi-stomped down the hall and returned with her phone, pure distaste on her face.

Cal cared, but not enough to do anything different. He navigated to her texts and found the string with Justin's name on it. He ignored the fact that it had a little heart next to the name.

"No last name?"

"Briggs," Sierra said in a bored voice.

Cal went to the top of the string, and he saw that his daughter had initiated the conversation with this boy. They were flirtatious, but he didn't see any foul language, no naked pictures, and nothing to suggest that he needed to take this phone from her for four years.

Heck, his texts with Lisa were probably more scandalous. She'd sent him a selfie of her at her desk earlier this week, and one of her in a bathing suit as she searched for a new one.

"Okay." He handed the phone back. "You can use it as an alarm clock. No texting after nine. If I see one text after nine…."

"I know, Dad." She took the phone, and he sensed her patience with him was almost gone.

They ate the rest of their ice cream in silence, and Cal wished he was better at coming up with something to talk about. As it was, his mind started circling around Lisa and if she was really fake and shallow. And if she wasn't, why had Sierra thought that?

———

Cal felt completely out of his element on the beach. Sure, he'd grown up on this island, and he loved the beach as much as the next Hawaiian. But he'd always come with a woman—his mother or his wife—and they carried bags with all the necessities for spending time in the sun. Sunscreen, towels, a hat, cold water.

He carried his towel over his arm, feeling foolish because Lisa hadn't shown up yet. He glanced down the beach, noting how busy this stretch had gotten since the food trucks had started gathering here on weekends. He could picture it from the perspective of a child, of his boyhood afternoons on this beach.

No paved parking lot. No restrooms. Just half a block from the house where he'd lived for six years, his brothers yelling at him to slow down as he ran down the path ahead of them. They carried nothing then, and he'd pull his shirt over his head as soon as he came out from under the trees and saw the whole world in front of him.

His mother would gather all the T-shirts for him and his brothers, and spread out their blankets, and have spam and egg sandwiches waiting for them when they finally dragged themselves out of the ocean.

Cal had loved beach afternoons with his younger brothers. He missed them powerfully in that moment, and he pulled out his phone to send them a quick text about this beach on their family string.

He smiled at the responses from Collin, then Cole, then Carter, and he laughed at the emojis his youngest brother used. He toyed with the idea of telling them that he'd started seeing Lisa, but his daughter's words about Lisa being shallow kept him from saying anything.

"Hey."

Cal jumped at the sound of Lisa's voice, as if she could see inside his head and know what troubled him.

"Hey." He laughed with her and threw his arm around her. She wore a gauzy, white coverup that her body heat easily came through.

"I hope you're hungry," she said. "Because I've eaten at all of these food trucks before, and they're fantastic."

Cal stepped back and looked at her, trying to see what his daughter had. Fake smile? Shallow because she wore diamond studs in her earlobes? Nice clothes? Cute sandals?

Cal didn't get any of those vibes from her, and he said, "I'm *really* hungry."

"Coconut shrimp?" she asked. "Fish tacos? Shaved ice?"

"Tacos first," he said. "Shaved ice with the fruit second."

"Oh, you like the fruit."

"I mean, it's not coffee and ice cream, but I do love the fresh fruit shaved ice."

"Me too." Lisa linked her arm through his. "Let's go find a spot first, okay? Then we can eat."

"I used to come to this beach as a kid," he said. "My family owned a house in the neighborhood right on the other side of the trees there, and we'd walk down all the time."

"Wow, nice. Must've been great for a boat maker, to be so close to the water."

"We did always grow up near water," Cal said. "When we left that house, we moved over by the cove on Lightning Point."

"I *love* that cove," Lisa said, dancing ahead of him. "It's the best snorkeling on the island."

"So they say."

"You don't like snorkeling?"

"I like it fine," he said.

"It's in my top five outdoor activities," Lisa said. "How's here?" She'd found a spot big enough for the two of them, and maybe one other person on each side, which meant no one would take that sand.

"Here's great." He spread his towel out, so glad to be rid of it finally. She set her bag on the towel and lay hers next to his, moving her bag to the middle of the space.

After digging out her wallet, she said, "Let's go."

Cal said, "I'll pay."

"Oh, you sure will," she said with that cute, coy smile he really liked. "I just don't want to leave my wallet unattended."

They got in line at the taco truck, and Lisa turned back to him. "Tell me about your brothers."

"What about them?"

"Married, single? What do they do?"

"You looking for a new boyfriend?" Cal asked, chuckling.

"No." Lisa pushed both hands against his chest, and

he put his arms around her. He didn't normally act like this in public, but he decided he didn't care how he normally did things. He'd worn that stupid shirt with the sailboats on it.

"Carter's working a fishing boat out of Anchorage," Cal said. "He's got a wife and a baby."

"Mm."

"Cole's still here on the island. He works as an accountant for the city. And Collin bought an avocado farm."

"An avocado farm?"

"I'm not even lying." Cal chuckled. "I'm the only one who loved the carpentry enough to learn it from my dad and go into business doing it."

"Well, I want some free avocados," she said, stepping up to the truck to order.

"Yeah, well, I'm still waiting for my dance," he said. "Sometimes we don't always get what we want."

"Oh, you'll get your dance," she said, stepping out of the way. "But we're having tacos first."

———

A FEW HOURS LATER, CAL HELPED LISA STAND. "I'M sorry," he said. "But I grounded Sierra, and I promised her I'd be home by five with dinner and a movie so we could spend some time together."

"I'm glad," she said. "This has been such a great day, hasn't it?"

"Great," he echoed. "Where'd you park?"

"I didn't," she said. "I got a ride with a friend from work."

"You had to work today?"

"Yeah, Deirdre has this high-needs bride, and the wedding is in two weeks, and we were there making sure everything is set for the final meeting on Monday."

Cal nodded. "You want a ride home?"

"Absolutely. I can't walk to the Avenues from here." She gave him a flirtatious smile that made his heart pound. All he could think about was kissing her when he dropped her off, and his hands felt slick on the steering wheel.

He managed to get down the road, make the right turns, and pull up to her house. Was this really where he was going to kiss her for the first time? Was that romantic? A middle-of-the-day kiss on her front porch?

"What about brunch tomorrow?" he asked when she didn't get out. "I'm not the best cook on the planet, but I can make poached eggs, and Sierra is great with toast and hash."

"What time?" she asked.

"Brunch time? Eleven?"

"I can make that work," she said. "Your place?"

"My place. I'll text you the address, okay?"

"Okay." She reached for the door handle, but Cal didn't want her to go yet.

His hand shot out and touched her arm. She turned back to him, a question in her blue, blue eyes. The moment heated, and he dropped his eyes to her lips. Nothing had to be said, and she leaned toward him in the same second he moved toward her.

He brushed his lips against her, his brain screaming at him to *get this right! Don't mess up!*

His hand slid up her neck and cradled her face, and the second time their lips touched, he held on as he kissed her. And while he still wasn't sure he was doing it right, kissing Lisa sure did feel amazing.

Chapter Eleven

Lisa could only feel Cal. Everything else fell completely away, leaving only the roughness of his hands on her face, the warmth from his mouth against hers, the scent of his cologne. He completely overwhelmed her, and when he pulled away, Lisa knew she'd just been kissed by a real man.

Wow, she thought.

"Yeah," Cal said. "Wow."

So maybe she'd spoken that word out loud. Her brain wasn't exactly operating at the moment, because he'd shorted it out with that electrifying kiss.

They breathed in and out together, the scent of leather and air freshener and his cologne filling her nose.

"Brunch tomorrow," he said, his voice a little husky.

"Yes," she confirmed again. She finally dared to lift her eyes to his, and in the next moment, they both laughed. The ice between them broke, and relief rushed through Lisa.

"I haven't kissed anyone in a long time," Cal admitted, wiping his hand down his face.

"Well, you'd never know," Lisa said.

"Yeah?" Cal looked at her with such hope in his eyes, and all Lisa wanted to do was kiss him again. So she did, this human connection so welcome and so wonderful. He made her heartbeat do things it had never done before, and her skin cells buzzed with an energy she'd never experienced.

"I better go," she whispered a few seconds later, and Cal settled back behind the wheel.

"Yeah, me too." He sighed and looked out the window. "Maybe you'd like to come hang out with me and my daughter sometime." He swung his attention back to her, and Lisa saw something there she wasn't sure about.

"Of course I would," she said. She knew that if she had any chance of winning Cal's heart, she'd have to win over Sierra too. "How did she—I mean, did she say anything about me?" She'd wanted to know what his daughter thought of her, but their first meeting hadn't lasted long. And it had been very tense.

She also didn't want Cal to feel like he had to tell her anything his daughter shared with him. "Never mind," she said, shaking her head. Her skin suddenly itched from being in the sand all day. "I don't need to know."

"Maybe next weekend," he said. "We can all go out

to Lightning Point. Or Shark's Reef. Or something. She likes to wakeboard."

"Next weekend…." Lisa tried to think through her calendar. She couldn't, her lips still tingling from that kiss. "I'll have to check my calendar and let you know. The weekend after that is the wedding."

"Right," he said.

"Okay, bye." She got out of the truck then and walked up to her front door. Inside, Suzy was already barking, but Lisa took a moment to turn back and wave to Cal. He lifted his hand too, and then started backing out of her driveway.

The new floor inside was still surprising, and Lisa bent down to scratch her dog. "Well, he kissed me, Suze." She giggled as she dropped her beach bag, made her way to the couch, and collapsed onto it with a happy sigh. "And it was amazing."

Suzy jumped up onto the couch and curled into Lisa's side. She absently stroked the animal as her mind wandered. Cal had not confirmed nor denied that Sierra had said anything about her.

"She probably didn't," Lisa said, getting up. "They probably talked about the new boyfriend and not me." At least she hoped that was what had happened. Her nerves took on another dose of energy, but this time it all came from anxiety.

Could she really be a mother to a fourteen-year-old girl? Sierra knew and remembered her mom. She would never think of Lisa as her mother.

She pulled out her phone and ordered dinner for herself. Normally, she hated being home on weekend nights alone, but usually because that meant she didn't have a date—again. But she'd just spent an amazing day with an amazing man, so she was fine to order her fried chicken and stay in for the evening.

As soon as her order had been confirmed, she dialed her mother.

"Sweetie," her mom said after the phone had only rung once. "I'm showing a house right now. Call you back?"

"Okay," Lisa said, and she'd barely gotten the second syllable out before the call ended. She sighed again, because she really needed to talk to her mother about well, being a mother.

Step one, she thought. *Be available.*

She couldn't really blame her mom. When Lisa's dad had left, her mother had to figure out how to support herself. She'd been married for almost forty years and never worked outside the home. She'd turned to real estate, and things on the island had been hopping lately.

Her food arrived the moment her mom called, and Lisa managed to take the bag of food and answer her phone in the span of a single second. "Hey, Mom," she said.

"Honey, how are you?" Her mother had a bit of drama in her, but Lisa supposed she did too.

"Great," she said. "Where are you showing right now?"

"There's a great five-bedroom in the gated community just outside town," she said, as if Lisa was in the market for a five-bedroom mansion.

"Wow," she said. "Many people stopping by?"

"A few, yes," she said. "At least at the end here. It was mostly neighbors in the beginning."

"Well, they have to keep an eye on their property values," Lisa said, putting her food on her kitchen counter. She switched her mother to speaker and started unpacking the bag. "Look, I called because...." Why had she called?

"Did you hear about Kylie?" her mother asked. "Because she was worried about how you'd take the news."

Lisa looked up as if her younger sister would be standing there, ready to tell her "the news."

"No," she said. "I haven't heard from Kylie."

"Really?" Her mother wore her frown in her voice. "She said she'd call you."

"When?"

"Oh, ages ago."

"She probably forgot." Her youngest sister thought a real career could be had on the Internet. Sure, Lisa knew there were people who made money with video channels and all of that, but her sister wasn't one of them, despite her best efforts. She wasn't exactly flighty, but she did move from idea to idea at the speed of sound.

"Well...she's engaged."

Lisa dropped the plate she'd just taken out of the

cupboard. Her heart had forgotten how to beat. "Engaged?" fell from her lips once the ear-splitting sound of the plate hitting the counter had stopped.

And now her cute, perky, blonde sister was engaged before her.

"She and Kyle are thrilled, of course," her mother said. "And we're thrilled for them. I mean, I know you are."

"Of course," Lisa said, looking around the house like it was an alien planet. Her older sister had been married for a couple of years now, and Lisa really wanted to be second. She was already the second sister, and there was something so much better about second than there was last.

Last.

The only one not married.

"Vic is throwing her a bridal shower in a few weeks."

"A few weeks?" Lisa asked. "When are they getting married?" She forgot that not everyone booked Your Tidal Forever for their nuptials, and not everyone took upwards of a year to plan the perfect wedding.

"Oh, not until September, but Vic is a little excited."

"Oh, yeah," Lisa said. "Me too." Her older sister loved throwing parties, and a bridal shower? Vic would've been on cloud nine since the announcement. The announcement Lisa had not gotten.

Her throat pinched, and she tried to tell herself that it was okay. Her sisters didn't deliberately leave her out.

Obviously, Kylie had spoken to their mother about making sure Lisa didn't feel bad. Excluded. Whatever.

She didn't know how she felt. She just knew she wanted this conversation to end. She knew she wanted to eat her fried chicken and mashed potatoes. And she knew she'd need a lot of ice cream to get through the evening alone.

Her mother had started talking again, but Lisa hadn't been listening. "Hey, Mom," she interrupted. "I'm so sorry, but I have to jet. Call from work."

"Oh, okay. Love you, sweetie."

"Love you too." Once again, Lisa's last word fell on a dead line, as her mother had already hung up. Lisa looked at her phone and then set it down on the kitchen counter. Robotically, she scooped her food onto a plate and went into the living room, where Suzy waited obediently on the couch.

With the TV on, she ate, feeding bits of chicken to her dog. She had no idea what she was watching, only that it numbed her mind enough so she wouldn't have to think.

"I'm so sorry I'm late," Lisa said the next day. She knew it was closer to eleven-thirty than the top of the hour, but her meeting with Deirdre that morning had run long. "There was so much to do at work this morning, and…." Her voice trailed off when she realized she'd left her purse in her office.

Twenty minutes across town from where she was currently turning a corner to go to Cal's house.

"And what?" he asked.

She shook her head. She didn't need her purse—unless she got pulled over. "And nothing. I'm two minutes away."

"Okay," he said. "I'll get everything hot again." He didn't sound upset, but Lisa's stomach clenched.

"I'm sorry," she said.

"We're fine, Lisa," he said. "See you in a minute." He hung up, and Lisa put both hands on the steering wheel. This brunch felt huge to her, and she wasn't even sure why.

She parked beside Cal in his driveway, noting how perfect his lawn looked, and how quaint and quiet the neighborhood was. The porch looked like it had been cared for by a feminine hand, and she knocked once before the front door opened.

Cal stood there wearing a pair of khaki pants and a shirt the color of watermelon skins. His dark beard was oh-so-sexy, and she remembered the scratch of it against her face. "Hey," she said, everything tense inside her releasing.

He smiled at her, and everything seemed right in the world. "Hey. Come on in." He stepped back, and Lisa entered to a small foyer. An office sat to her right, with a hallway in front of her.

"Kitchen's back here," he said, starting that way. She tried not to worry that he hadn't kissed her or taken her hand in his. She followed him past a small bathroom and into the kitchen, dining room, and living room.

"Oh, the windows are great," she said, basking in the tropical light that came from the back and sides of the room.

Sierra looked up from the island, where she worked with a knife.

Lisa kept her smile in place. "What are you making?" she asked.

"Just chopping some parsley," the teen said. No smile. Barely looking at Lisa before focusing on the herbs on the cutting board.

"We have poached eggs and toast," Cal said, opening the oven. "Sierra cut up some fruit, and we got a bunch of grapefruits from our trees and juiced them." He put a sheet pan with food on the counter beside Sierra and turned to the fridge.

The beautiful, pink liquid shone in the glass pitcher, and Lisa smiled at it. "Wow, that's beautiful."

Sierra made a noise, and Lisa looked at her. She wasn't sure if it was a scoff or a laugh or a sigh—or nothing at all. She still steadily chopped the herbs, and Lisa thought they'd be pesto before long.

"Bug," Cal said, something cool in his voice. "I think they're good."

Sierra stopped chopping and looked at her father. So much was said between the two of them, just like last night. Lisa didn't like not being included, but she was the newcomer here. She looked back and forth between them, and Cal finally said, "I think we're ready."

"Forks, Dad," Sierra said, and Cal opened a drawer in front of him.

Three forks on the counter later, and he said, "Now we're ready." He smiled at Lisa and Sierra and reached for a plate. He handed it to Lisa, which made her feel warm and welcome, and he scooped up an open-faced egg sandwich and put it on her plate.

Sierra sprinkled a little parsley on it and added, "There's a sort of hollandaise on the stove, if you want that."

Lisa did want a rich sauce for her brunch, and she stepped around the counter to get it.

"Juice?" Cal asked.

"Yes, please," she said. They danced in the kitchen, each of them getting their food before heading over to the table, which had windows on two sides of it.

Lisa sighed as she sat, and Cal asked, "Rough morning at work?"

"There's just a lot of little pieces to work through," she said. She cut into her poached egg, and only a little bit of yolk ran out.

"I told you they'd be overdone," Sierra said, her own egg yolk not running at all.

"It's fine," Cal said, putting a bite of toast and egg in his mouth. His eyes didn't agree with what his mouth had said though, and Lisa looked at Sierra.

"What do you like to do, Sierra?" she asked. "Are you on any teams? Clubs?"

The girl looked at her with those big hazel eyes, and she wondered what her mother had looked like. "I like to eat on time," she said.

"Sierra," Cal said sharply.

"What?" Sierra got up and took her plate into the kitchen. "This isn't even good anymore. Can I make a sandwich?" She didn't wait for Cal to give his permission before she opened the trashcan and dumped her breakfast into it.

"I'm sorry," Lisa said to the whole house, her chest hitching. She looked at Cal helplessly.

"It's fine," he said, calmly cutting another bite and putting it in his mouth. Sierra indeed made a sandwich and returned to the table. Her phone chimed, and Cal glared at her. "We don't eat with—"

"Holy cow, Dad." She held up her phone for him to look at it. He took it from her and adjusted how close it was to his face.

"Prom?"

"Can I go?"

"Who is this boy?" He looked at Sierra. "It's not Travis, and it's not Justin."

"That's Mikel," she said. "You know, the boy down at the end of the street? We've been friends forever with the Palou's."

"Mikel Palou," he repeated. "He's fourteen."

"Yep."

"So his parents would drive you to the prom." Cal looked at Lisa, as if she was going to give him any advice in this situation.

"Probably." Sierra took her phone back. "Can I go with him?"

"When is it?"

"April thirtieth."

"He asked you over a text," Cal said, clearly disgusted. Lisa had to agree with him on that, but she reminded herself that she and Cal were from a different generation than Sierra and Mikel.

"Yeah, and he's cute, and we're already friends." Sierra looked at Cal with so much hope in her eyes. Lisa would've said yes in a heartbeat.

"The thirtieth is five days after my two-week grounding ends," she said. "Please, Dad?"

Cal looked at Lisa again and back to his daughter. "All right. But I want a full itinerary. I want to know what you're wearing and what he's wearing and who else you'll be with."

Sierra squealed and jumped up from the table to hug him. "Thanks, Dad." She started tapping on her phone a mile a minute, her bad eggs as well as the sandwich she'd made clearly forgotten.

"You'll need a dress," Lisa said. "Have you bought a prom dress before?"

"No," Sierra said without looking up.

"I know the best places on the island," Lisa said. "If you're interested, I can give you the names of the shops."

Sierra did look at her then. "I'm sure I can find something at the mall."

"Oh, okay," Lisa said, not quite sure why this girl didn't like her. Cal had said he'd made a promise to his late wife to find someone else to grow old with. He'd said Sierra was fine with him starting to date.

But apparently, not with him dating Lisa.

She gave the teenager a tight smile and went back to her rubbery egg. It really wasn't good, and it probably would've been had she been on time. She sighed and put down her fork, looked at Cal, and tried to smile.

It didn't quite work. He reached over and covered her hand with his, a silent show that he didn't mind that she'd been late.

But his daughter certainly did, and Sierra left the table a moment later. "I'm going to call Megan," she said. "Maybe her mom can give us a ride to the mall today."

"I can take you," Cal said.

"I'll ask her," Sierra said, walking through the kitchen and down another hall, where the bedrooms clearly were.

"Well, that was a disaster," Lisa said as soon as she was gone. "She doesn't like me much, does she?"

"She's fourteen," Cal said. "She doesn't know what she likes."

Lisa might not have had a lot of experience with teens, but she knew the cold shoulder when she got it.

"I mean, this is the third boy she'll be going out with

this month," Cal said darkly. "She goes by how she feels in the moment."

Lisa nodded and helped him clean up the kitchen. "I really am sorry I was late."

"I know." He took her into his arms. "I'm glad you're here. You want to go for a walk up to the waterfall?"

"Mm, yes," she said, some of the pressure off her shoulders now that she was alone with him.

"Okay, but first." Cal smiled and kissed her, and Lisa decided she could put up with surly teenagers if she got to kiss Cal Lewiston afterward.

Chapter Twelve

C al's phone was blowing up, and he knew who it was. Sierra.

School had been out for an hour or two, and he still had another couple to go before he'd be home. He'd already given her permission to go shopping with her friends after school, despite her grounding. With only ten more days until the prom, she still didn't have a dress, and the situation was "dire." Her words, not his.

He pulled off his kneepads, said, "I need a minute," and pulled out his phone as he stepped outside of the house he was working on. Sure enough, Sierra had texted eight times, all about the fruitlessness of finding a decent dress he would approve of.

The last three texts were pictures, and none of them were appropriate for a fourteen-year-old freshman in high school to wear to her first prom.

What do you think of those? she'd asked, and Cal felt like an ogre for wanting to veto all of them. But he supposed a few years of ogre-dom was what he'd signed up for when he'd become a father.

The blue one has no sleeves or straps. We already talked about that.

The pink one looks like it would barely cover your bottom half. So that was totally out.

And the black one—does that V-neck go down to your belly button?

Sierra started typing immediately, and her response was *Dad.*

What? he thumbed out. *None of these are appropriate.*

It's all there is!

He tapped the phone icon and lifted his device to his ear.

"What?" his daughter practically barked at him.

"First, you talk to me like that again, and you won't be leaving the house until Christmas." Cal could be grumpy too if he had to be.

"I'm sorry," she said quickly, and she sounded like she was too. "I'm just frustrated. I don't know where to find a dress."

He looked up into the brilliant blue sky, this job cleaning up after the tsunami almost finished. No one else had contacted him, as the island was mostly put back together now.

"I know, baby," he said with a sigh. "Why don't you

text Lisa? She really does know what she's talking about. She works at the premier wedding planner on the island."

Silence came through the line. Every time he brought up Lisa, Sierra rewarded him with silence. After their brunch last weekend, where Lisa had been late, Sierra had once again called her fake.

Did you see that smile? Sierra had shaken her head and rolled her eyes. *Fake.*

Cal had seen it. Maybe it was a little on the professional side instead of the personal side, but he saw the other, softer side of her too. The side where she stood in her hallway, her foot dripping blood. The side where she pounded out the drywall in her house. The side where she finished his drink and asked him to dance. They still hadn't done that.

"Fine," Sierra said. "Will you send me her number?"

"Really?" Cal asked.

"I need a dress, Dad."

"Okay, well, she has a huge wedding this weekend. Be really polite, okay? Like, over-the-top polite."

"I will."

"I'll know if you're not."

"Dad," Sierra said. "I can be polite."

Cal didn't want to get into an argument right now. "I just...you've never really been nice to her, bug." Not at the outdoor cinema. Not during brunch. And not during movie night this past Saturday evening. In fact, she'd only stayed for twenty minutes of the movie before asking Cal if she could just go to her room.

Her grounding ended on Sunday, and Cal worried he shouldn't have even let her go shopping after school. But he couldn't take her to do everything, and his indecision and guilt had allowed him to give her permission to do prom-related things after school, as long as he knew exactly where she was and who she was with.

"I'll be nice to her," Sierra promised. "Or you can take the prom from me."

Cal knew how important this was to his daughter. "All right. I'll text you her number."

"Thanks, Dad. We'll head home now, and I'll get dinner started."

"Okay, that would be great. I'm probably still two hours out."

"Okay." Sierra hung up, and Cal quickly typed out Lisa's phone number and sent it to Sierra. Then he sent Lisa a quick message, telling her that he'd given her number to Sierra, and that his daughter needed help with finding an appropriate prom dress. Heavy emphasis on *appropriate*.

Really? Lisa sent back.

Really really, he messaged her.

Great. I'll hook her up with something awesome. A smiley face emoji followed, and Cal turned back to the house. If he could get the rest of the floor finished, this place would be done. He and his crew would only have four more houses to finish, and their deadline sat only three days in the future.

So he couldn't knock off early, and he went back inside, strapped on his kneepads, and got back to work.

———

WHEN HE ENTERED THE HOUSE WITH "SEA, I'M HOME," the scent of hamburgers met his nose. His stomach twisted, because he was starving, and she'd made his favorite food. At the same time, he wondered what she wanted.

"Dad," she said over her shoulder from where she stood at the stove. "The fries just have a few more minutes."

Burgers and fries. Sierra definitely wanted something. He backtracked to his office and dropped his bag with paperwork on the desk. He kicked off his boots and headed back into the kitchen in his socks.

He soaped up to his elbows in the sink and took a bottle of water out of the fridge. "All right," he said. "What's going on?"

"Going on?" Sierra reached for a roll of paper towels, and she made a little bed of them on a plate before spooning the perfectly golden and crisp French fries onto it. "Nothing's going on."

Right. "Did you talk to Lisa?"

"Yes."

"And?" He really wasn't in the mood for games and

cryptic conversations tonight. He was exhausted, and he and Adam had agreed to meet at seven o'clock in the morning to get an early start on one of the four remaining homes. The owners were out of town, and if they started early, they'd have a better chance of making their deadline.

"And you were right. She's really busy with the wedding this weekend."

"So she can't text you the names of the shops?"

"She did."

"Sea," he said. "I need you to just tell me what's going on."

She set the plate of fries on the counter and salted them. "Let's eat," she said. "And I'll tell you." She smiled at him, and in that moment, with his daughter in a good mood and minimal makeup, he remembered the little girl she'd once been. Love moved through him powerfully, and he smiled back at her.

"All right." He fixed up his burger with all the things he liked, because Sierra had made sure to make them all, right down to the fried egg. They sat at the table, and he said, "Start talking."

"Lisa gave me the names of a few dress shops," she said. "But they all require appointments."

"Okay." He took another bite of his burger, hoping he wouldn't choke on the food with whatever his daughter said next.

"Some of them are booked out already," Sierra said. "Like, I can't even get in before the prom." She dipped a fry through some ketchup. "So I called Lisa and asked her what to do. She said she could get us in."

Sierra had called Lisa. And neither of them had texted him, so the conversation must've gone okay. "And?" he asked.

"Lisa is very busy," Sierra said. "Until next week, which is too late. She called around to all the shops, and we have two appointments...tonight."

"Tonight?"

"And I know I'm grounded and all of that, but this is prom-related, and I really want to go. I can't get the appointments by myself, and there's no time, and can I please go?"

"What time is the first appointment?"

"Uh, twenty minutes." Sierra took a bite of her burger. "Lisa should be here any minute."

Any minute? "Why didn't you text me?"

"Because you're super busy too, and I figured it would be okay, because it's Lisa and she's your girl-friend." She lifted her eyebrows. "Right? She is your girl-friend, isn't she?"

"Yes," Cal said. "And you can go with her. Do you want me to come?"

"Uh, no." Sierra smiled at him. "I love you, but no. Lisa will send you pictures."

The doorbell rang, and Luna barked as she went skidding toward the door. She came trotting back, clearly torn between begging for a bite of hamburger and attacking the serial killer who'd dared to ring the doorbell.

Sierra got up and stuffed another bite into her mouth. Cal followed her to find her giving Lisa a quick hug in the doorway. Surprise darted through him, because literally that morning, Sierra wouldn't have anything to do with Lisa.

"Hey," Lisa said, stepping past Sierra to kiss Cal quickly. "Sierra explained to me all your rules for modesty. I promise to send you pictures."

"I'll be in the car," Sierra said, making a quick escape.

"Why is she so jumpy?" Cal asked.

"I think she's worried about price," Lisa said. "But I'll get her our discount." She flashed him a brilliant smile and emitted a little squeal. "Can you believe she called me? I'm so excited."

"You tell me if she's not nice. Even a tiny little bit, Lisa." He squeezed her hand. "Okay? That was part of my deal with her."

"She's been awesome," Lisa said. "Kind, and polite." She beamed at him. "You and Jo have done a great job with her."

"Thank you," Cal said, an automatic response. Before Jo's death, she'd done most of the raising of their daughter.

"I'll stay in touch," Lisa said, grinning. "We'll be late if we don't leave now." She kissed him again quickly, and

Cal held the door as she left. He waved to his daughter and went to finish his dinner.

And after that…he'd put his phone on his chest so he could hear it when it chimed, and he'd take a nap.

"Please let them get along," he whispered. "Okay, Jo? Maybe now would be a good time to let Sierra know it's okay to like Lisa."

Chapter Thirteen

Lisa got behind the wheel of her car, wondering what in the world to say to a fourteen-year-old girl. Then she realized she dealt with women like Sierra all the time. Maybe a decade or two older, but in the exact same position.

"So, tell me what kind of dress you're dreaming about." She put the car in reverse and backed out of Cal's driveway. Her giddiness was a little ridiculous, but she didn't care. She'd been thinking about having a serious conversation with Cal about his daughter and how she might come between them.

Maybe now, she wouldn't have to.

"I think I look good in blue," Sierra said. "Or black. Something a little darker."

"So no pink or yellow or like, light blue."

"Ew, no." Sierra shook her head, and Lisa thought she'd actually look good in something pink, because her hair was dark. But she knew better than most that what looked the best was what felt the most comfortable to the person wearing it.

"We're meeting with a woman named Amarillis. She's been a dress consultant for a long time, and I'm sure you're going to love her."

"What does a dress consultant do?"

"She'll measure you and ask you what you like. Then she'll pull dresses for you to try on."

"So I can't just look?"

"Sure, you can," she said. "But it's not browsing." She glanced at Sierra. "You have to let her take care of you. They'll offer you a drink, and I can help you in the dressing room, or Rilla can."

"I can put on a dress," Sierra said.

"Okay," Lisa said, because she didn't want to argue with her. But she wouldn't be able to put on these dresses. They weren't department store dresses, and she'd need at least a little bit of help.

A few minutes later, she pulled up to a building that looked like it should be condemned and said, "Here we are."

"Are you sure?" Sierra looked out the windshield at the nondescript building with no signage and only two other cars in the lot.

"Yep." She opened her door and got out. "And let's go. We barely have a minute to spare."

Sierra joined her, and Lisa opened the door to the dress shop, the sight of all the dresses spreading before her making her pulse quicken the tiniest bit. "We get a lot of our bridesmaids dresses here," she explained as she removed her sunglasses and balanced them on her head.

"Wow," Sierra said, pausing just inside the door.

Rilla came toward them, a huge smile on her face. "Lisa," she said with a laugh. "How are you?" She hugged Lisa, who also giggled.

"So great," she said, backing up. "This is Sierra Lewiston. She needs the perfect prom dress."

"Nice to meet you, Sierra," Rilla said, so perfectly poised and professional. Her dark auburn hair fell in waves over her shoulders, and Lisa had literally never seen her without a smile. "What can I get you guys to drink?"

"I want that lemonade you guys have here," Lisa said.

Rilla shook her head with another laugh. "I put one in the freezer when you called so it would be cold." She looked at Sierra. "Water? Soda? Lemonade?"

"I'm fine," she said, and Lisa wished she'd told her to take the drink. She wasn't sure why, but she was always more relaxed when Riley—or now Sunny—had managed to get a drink for her clients before they came back. She supposed she just liked the personal touch.

Rilla bustled off to get her lemonade, and Lisa stepped next to Sierra. "I see a lot of black and blue right now. And red. Look at that one." She pointed to a red dress in the left corner of the shop. "What are you thinking for sleeves? Length?"

"My dad says it has to have sleeves," she said. "Wide straps, nothing spaghetti-like."

"I wonder what he'd think of a cap sleeve," Lisa said.

"He'd freak out," Sierra said dryly. "I swear, sometimes I think he thinks I'm still four."

Lisa's heart skipped a beat. "Who knows what he thinks?"

Sierra blinked at Lisa. "Wow. I wasn't expecting that."

"What were you expecting?"

"I don't know. You to tell me he just loves me. Just wants the best for me."

He does, Lisa thought, but she kept those words cooped up in her mind. "You don't need advice from me."

Rilla returned and handed Lisa the frosty lemonade bottle. Her mouth watered as she twisted the lid, as Rilla said, "Okay, Sierra. Tell me what you like." She led her further into the shop, and Lisa sipped her lemonade while they picked out a few dresses to try on.

She learned quickly that Sierra wanted something long, though they got a shorter one in a nice shade of burgundy just to try. Rilla's assistant hung all their choices in a dressing room, and finally, Rilla said, "I think we have some really good options. Should we try on?"

"Yes." Sierra looked from her to Lisa, clearly not even sure where the fitting rooms were.

"I'll hold your purse," Lisa said, taking it from the teen. "You go with Rilla." She followed, because there were comfortable armchairs in front of the dressing rooms, and she needed to be able to take pictures for Cal.

She'd already snapped a few on the sly, and she texted them to him while she waited.

"Uh, Lisa?" Sierra's voice came from the room where she'd gone.

"Yeah?"

"I need some help." She pulled back the curtain, and she was practically falling out of her dress.

Lisa launched herself out of the armchair and over to Sierra. "Turn and let me see." Sierra did, and sure enough, the sleeve was all bunched and twisted from how she'd put it on. "Okay, this needs to go here...." She fixed it and finished zipping up the dress.

Sierra looked up and at herself in the mirror, and Lisa's whole heart melted. "What are you going to do with your hair?" she managed to ask without sounding like she was emotional.

"My friend is going to curl it and pin it all up."

Lisa gently gathered Sierra's hair and lifted it so she could see the dress without her hair covering her shoulders. "It's really pretty."

"I don't know if I like the skirt," she said, brushing at the blue fabric. "It doesn't lay right or something."

"Let's take a picture and show your father."

Sierra smiled and gave the peace sign; Lisa clicked and texted. Cal must've been glued to his phone, because his response was instant.

WOW.

"All caps," Lisa said with a smile. "Wow."

Sierra turned and twisted, looking at herself, and finally said, "Let's try the black one."

She put it on, and the huge billowy skirt required a second skirt to be worn underneath. Lisa stepped out to get one, and she helped Sierra put it on underneath the dress.

"Oh," Lisa said, because this dress took her breath away.

"It has straps," Sierra said, staring at herself in wonder.

"Smile," Lisa said, and she took another picture. She sent that one to Cal, noticing that Sierra wasn't doing the self-examination this time. Lisa knew why. She'd seen that look on her bride's faces too.

"The red one?" she asked anyway, because they were here, and she might as well try on as many dresses as she wanted until she was convinced that silky, flowing, wide-skirted dress was "the one."

Four dresses later, and many texts with Cal, Sierra came out of the dressing room back in her regular clothes.

"So?" Lisa asked, her eyebrows raised. She was beyond ready to get out of these wedges, but she would never show it. She needed to stop by Riley's place to make sure everything was still standing and working and all of that, but she'd never tell Sierra that either.

"I think the black one," she said slowly, hurrying to

add, "But it's so much, and I need that second set of skirts, and I still need shoes…."

"Did your father give you a budget?" Lisa asked.

"Well, kind of." Sierra bit her fingernail, and Lisa simply couldn't have her worried about this.

"Sierra, this is your first prom. Let me give you a little advice when it comes to men and shopping."

The girl looked up at her, keen interest in her eyes. "Yeah?"

"You ask forgiveness, not permission." She grinned at her. "So let's tell Rilla we want the black one. And I trust you will find the perfect pair of red heels to wear with that dress."

"Red heels? Really?"

"Uh, yeah." Lisa nodded at her and turned as Rilla approached. "She wants the black one."

"Oh, that's the one I was hoping you'd get." Rilla clapped her hands a couple of times, and Lisa would've never known if Rilla actually liked the black one the best or not. "Whoever your date is, he's the luckiest guy on the island."

Sierra ducked her head, her smile filling her whole face. It took several minutes to get the discount worked out, buy the dress, and get it into the back of Lisa's car. She sighed like she'd just climbed to the top of the volcano on the northeast side of the island.

"Well," she said. "That was fun. Thanks for asking me to help you." She started the quick drive back to Cal's.

"It was fun," Sierra finally said. "You know, you're not as fake as I thought you were."

Lisa felt like someone had reached right into her lungs and snuffed the air out of them. "Oh…okay."

"My dad didn't tell you?"

Lisa shot her a quick glance, her chest barely able to expand. "Tell me that you thought I was fake? No, he didn't mention it."

Sierra's face colored again. "I just…it's…my mom—you can't tell my dad I said that. He'll take the dress away."

Lisa swallowed through a very narrow throat. "I won't mention it." After all, he hadn't mentioned what his daughter had said. She wore the professional clothes to be professional. And it wasn't a crime to like cute shoes. Was it? So she liked having manicured nails and wearing jewelry. Also not worth calling the police over.

She pulled into the driveway, and Cal came down the front steps while Sierra was still wrestling with the dress in the backseat.

"How'd it go?" he asked, and Lisa had no choice but to get out of the car. Well, she could've run him over, but she didn't think that would end well.

"Fine," she said, folding her arms across her stomach. She hadn't eaten dinner, and her feet hurt, and she decided on the spot to check Riley's house another time. It had survived the tsunami just fine because it was situated at a higher elevation, up in the rain forested hills.

"Hey, nugget." He gave his daughter a quick kiss on

the forehead. "I'll be right in and you can model for me, okay?"

"Dad."

"No arguing," he said. "Fashion show!"

Sierra rolled her eyes, but Cal turned back to Lisa, all smiles. "Thank you. Really. I kinda have no idea what I'm doing when it comes to stuff like this."

"It was fun," she said.

Cal cocked his head, those eyes searching for something she didn't want him to find.

"I have to go," she said.

"Why are you talking in that voice?"

"What voice?"

"It was fun," he repeated, his voice a few pitches higher. "That one. What happened?"

Lisa glanced toward the house, because she suddenly felt trapped between a rock and a hard place. She wanted to be honest with Cal. She liked him more than any other man she'd been out with in a long time.

The guy she'd dated last year—Richard—had broken up with her a couple of weeks before her family's holiday parties, claiming he didn't want to go because then they'd "be serious."

And Cal was serious, and Lisa didn't want to find out he thought she was fake too.

"Lisa?" He put his hand on her arm, and Lisa looked at it. Analyzed the way heat spread up her arm toward her shoulder, like someone had rubbed warm honey over her skin.

"She thinks I'm fake," she finally said, looking right into Cal's concerned eyes.

His widened, and a dangerous, hard glint entered them. "She said that?"

"She actually said I'm not as fake as she thought I was." Lisa watched him, and he was definitely not happy. "Did she tell you I was fake?"

When he didn't immediately deny it, Lisa's hopes—and the self-confidence she'd worked so hard to get back—plummeted.

Chapter Fourteen

C al had no idea what to say. Why had his daughter told Lisa that? Did she not have any tact whatsoever?

"She mentioned it after the outdoor cinema," he said very slowly. "I didn't know what to think of it, because I don't think you're fake."

"You don't?" She cocked eyebrow at one him, those arms still folded across her midsection.

"No," he said. "I mean, I didn't."

"You do now?"

"No." He sighed, frustrated. "I just—I guess I thought about it for a few seconds. I didn't see what she'd seen. That's all." He had a vision of this woman walking right out of his life, and he didn't want that to happen.

Surprising as that was, he really didn't want to be alone again. *You're not alone*, he thought. *You have Sierra.*

But in reality, he did sleep alone. Went to bed alone.

Shouldered all adult responsibilities alone. And he was tired.

"All right," Lisa finally said. "What are you doing for lunch tomorrow?"

"I have no idea. Probably eating the sandwich I make for myself every day."

"Maybe we could have lunch."

"Aren't you slammed with that wedding?"

Lisa sighed, her shoulders moving up and down very noticeably. "Yeah, I am. I'll have to check my schedule." She inched forward and took his hand in hers. "I just want to see you." She glanced toward the house. "Alone."

Cal wasn't sure he could sneak away from his job, as he had a deadline to meet. His crew could probably cover him for an hour. "I'll try," he said. "Text me." He drew her fully into his arms and bent his head close to hers. "I'm sorry she said you were fake. You're not, you know."

Lisa curled her hands around the back of his neck. "What am I then?"

"Gorgeous," he whispered. "Smart. Witty. Well-connected when it comes to shopping."

She giggled, and Cal could only hope that meant she'd forgiven him for whatever she'd thought he'd said or done about her being fake.

"I sure do like you, Lisa," he said, deciding he could bring back some of his old dating techniques. He kissed her before she could respond, and she kissed him back like she sure did like him too.

As she got in her car and backed out, Cal lifted his hand in a good-bye gesture, wondering how he'd ever lived without her in his life. The thought terrified him, because he didn't want to think he couldn't survive alone.

He'd gone through months of those debilitating feelings in the months following Jolene's death. Somehow, he and Sierra had come out the other side of that dark time, and they were both still alive. But Cal honestly had stretches of time he couldn't even remember.

"We're okay, right, Jo?" He gazed up into the sky, finding it several different shades of red, orange, yellow, and pink. The Hawaiian sunsets couldn't be beat, but tonight, the glorious sky didn't bring him much peace.

"I can't hear your voice anymore," he whispered. "I don't know how you smell." He missed his wife so much, and Cal didn't want to be disloyal to her, or her memory.

He should also probably stop talking to her if he really wanted to be serious with Lisa. So he turned around and went inside the house, wishing there was a manual for how to date after the death of a spouse.

"Okay," he said upon closing the door and finding Sierra on the couch, her nose buried in her phone. "First, the fashion show. And second, you're going to tell me what in the *world* possessed you to tell Lisa you thought she was fake."

———

THE NEXT DAY, CAL DID MANAGE TO SNEAK AWAY FROM the job site for lunch. Lisa had not texted, even when he had, asking what time would work for her. He told himself her silence was nothing. She was busy. She couldn't text him back the moment she got a message.

Never mind that she had before, even during busy times. Or maybe Cal didn't know what a busy time for Lisa was. They had only been dating for a few weeks.

His argument with Sierra last night had been a bit on the epic side, and in the end, they'd left it alone so they could each cool off. She'd been mad Lisa had told him, because she'd said she wouldn't. He was mad his daughter was so tactless as to tell a woman she was fake, even if she'd thought it one time and didn't anymore.

He'd asked her flat out if Sierra had a problem with him dating, and she'd said no. "So it's just me dating *her*," he'd said, trying to understand.

"I don't know, Dad," Sierra said, and Cal had been able to feel her frustration. Keenly. Because he didn't know either.

Maybe things between him and Lisa were moving too fast. That thought felt like one of the truest ones he'd had in a while, and he seized onto it.

He drove through a salad shop he knew Lisa liked and headed over to Your Tidal Forever. He felt very boyfriend-like as he walked in, carrying food for the two of them.

"Hello," a woman said with a bright voice and perfectly styled hair. She reminded him of Lisa, and yes, he found this woman a little fake. Maybe it was the ultra-white teeth. Who had teeth that color?

"Sir?"

He shook himself out of his thoughts. "Yes, I'm here for Lisa Ashford?"

"She's on a conference call," the woman said. "I'll let her know you're here." She gestured to a white couch. "You can wait right there if you'd like."

"Thanks," Cal said, moving over to the furniture. The sofa barely looked like it would hold him up, and it was also blindingly white, as if no one had ever waited here before.

"Cal," someone said, but it wasn't the feminine voice he wanted to hear.

He glanced up to find Hope Sorenson standing there, smiling at him. "Hey," he said, quickly standing to greet her. She gave him a side-hug, and Cal returned her smile.

"What are you doing here?" she asked, glancing at the bags of food he'd put on the floor.

"Oh, I'm dating Lisa," he said. "I brought her lunch, hoping she'd have a few minutes."

Hope's eyebrows shot toward the stars. "You're seeing Lisa?" Why she'd said it with so much surprise in her tone, Cal wasn't sure.

"Yes."

"Good for you," she said. "Finally getting out to date."

Before Cal could answer—and honestly, he didn't even know how—the woman went back down the hall.

"Oh, Sunny," Hope said, and Cal couldn't think of a better name for the blonde woman with the quick smile. "I need the Carmichael file."

"Sure thing, Miss Sorenson," Sunny said, turning to the row of filing cabinets behind her.

Hope took the file and turned back to Cal. "Good to see you, Cal."

"You too, Hope," he said, no "Miss Sorenson" in sight. He watched her go, wondering when he'd have time to work on another custom project for the wedding planning service.

"You're Cal?" Sunny asked, and Cal's idea to flop back onto the couch dissipated.

"Yes," he said slowly.

"That driftwood piece was exquisite," she said, her face shining. "I showed it to Riley. You know Riley, right? The girl who used to do my job? Anyway, I showed it to her, and she said she had to have it for her wedding."

Cal did indeed know who Riley Randall was, but he didn't know she was getting married. When he mentioned that, Sunny said, "Oh, they don't have a date yet. You know she's dating Evan Garfield, right? He's in Georgia Panic, and he is *so* dreamy." She continued talking, and Cal got the impression she could carry on a conversation with a post.

She finally stopped talking, and Cal did sit back down on the white couch. The minutes ticked by, and his impatience grew with each one. After about twenty minutes, he got up and said, "I'm just going to take this back."

He didn't wait for Sunny's permission, though she tried to protest. Her words fell on deaf ears as he went down the hall. He'd never been here as Lisa's boyfriend before, but he knew where her office was. He'd sat in meetings in her office before, and in that moment, Cal wondered why he'd never asked her out.

Of course, he'd never asked anyone out before her. His thoughts started to spiral, and he started second-guessing everything that had happened since the company's spring party.

Lisa's door was closed, but he knocked as he entered. She was on the phone, looking down at something on her desk. He could just leave the salad and go. He wouldn't have time to eat, and salad was particularly hard to eat in the car.

She glanced up as he approached, and he shook his head. Holding up the bag, he finished the walk to her desk and set it down. A smile came across her face, and she said, "Right, yes. We need the number nineteen stain for that...yes, I'll make sure we order enough." She rolled her eyes, and Cal could only smile back at her.

He set her bag of food down and turned to go, waving at her as he went.

"Can you hold on a sec, Ginger?" she asked. "I just need two minutes with my carpenter."

Cal turned back to her, and Lisa had risen. "You got me the nuts and berries," she said, fondness in her voice.

"I know you like that one," he said. "Sorry, I've been waiting for a while, and I have to get back to work too."

"I know." She groaned. "Sorry." She really looked like she was too.

"It's okay," he said. "Look, I know you only have a minute, but I wanted to talk to you about something." He pressed his fingertips together, trying to get his brain to slow down a little.

Slow down.

That was what he wanted to do. Slow down.

"I feel like maybe we're moving really fast," he said, suddenly too much saliva in his mouth. He swallowed. "I...need to go a little slower."

Lisa's eyebrows went up. "You think we're moving too fast?"

He shrugged. "I don't know. I—this is my first time dating in a long time."

She nodded, her expression guarded now. "I understand."

Cal wasn't sure, but she seemed like she actually didn't understand. And what was there to understand anyway?

"Thank you for the food," she said, and she went back around her desk. "All right, Ginger. I'm back."

Cal watched her for another few seconds, because he had the very distinct feeling that he'd just done something very wrong.

But he did need to go slow. He had to consider his daughter's feelings. He had to make sure he was ready to take the next step before he just went ahead and did it. And most of all, he had to decide if he was ready to be in a serious, committed relationship with another woman. Another woman who wasn't Jo.

His head pounded by the time he got back to his job site, and he stayed in the car to eat the Cobb salad he'd gotten for himself. This was familiar. Being alone actually soothed him. His thoughts quieted, leaving just one question behind: *Where does that leave me and Lisa?*

Chapter Fifteen

Lisa had never been happier to have a stack of folders on her desk than she was after Cal had showed up with the words, *I need to go a little slower.*

Slower.

Lisa scoffed as she checked the calendar notification that had just popped up on her phone. She couldn't wait until this wedding was over. She felt like her name would be in the headlines if something didn't go exactly as planned for the mayor's daughter.

Regina Keani was a nice woman, but wow, she had too many opinions on her dress, the flowers, the stationery, the altar, even the exact grain size of sand she wanted for her wedding. She'd paid to have bagged sand brought in so it wouldn't be full of "nasty critters" from the ocean.

And Your Tidal Forever did whatever it took to ensure the bride got the wedding of her dreams.

Lisa had thought she was getting closer to her own dream wedding. Then Cal had walked in with a big salad and the words *I need to go slower.*

Slower.

In Lisa's opinion, they were already moving extremely slow. She only saw him a couple of times a week, not every evening. She'd only met his daughter a couple of times, and not under the best of circumstances.

She felt like Cal had said *I want to break-up,* and her heart trembled inside her chest. Her phone rang, and she picked it up to see Deirdre's name on the screen. "What's up?" she asked after answering the call.

"I need you in my office," she said. "I have the florist on the line, and I think she has the wrong flowers."

"Oh, this is not happening," Lisa said, getting up quickly and heading for the door. "Be right there."

Deirdre was one of two new consultants Hope had hired about nine months ago. She was capable and smart, but she was still learning all the ropes at Your Tidal Forever. She'd been the junior consultant on the Keani wedding from the beginning, and it was a killer first file to be assigned to.

Lisa supposed she'd probably learned more in the last nine months than Lisa had in the three years she was a junior consultant. Didn't lessen the panic coming from Deirdre's eyes when Lisa walked into her office.

"...I just don't think those are right. Lisa is here." She turned her computer screen, where she had a video call going. Her wide eyes didn't instill any confidence into Lisa, but she focused on the screen instead.

"Those are gardenias and stephanotis," Lisa said. "That's not the Keani wedding. That's for the Chief of Police's daughter, Jennifer." She leaned closer and saw dozens of white flowers. "So those are ours. Just not for the Keani's." She looked at Deirdre and put her hand over hers.

"Oh, the Gardner wedding is two days before," the woman on the screen said. "Yes, okay. Phew. I really thought we'd ordered the wrong thing." She laughed, and Lisa was glad there hadn't been a problem. Thea at Petals & Leis was their go-to girl for flowers, and Lisa needed to be able to depend on her.

"Now, we should have dozens and dozens of roses for Regina," Lisa said. "Red and pink. They cover the altar, and that thing is not little. And calla lilies for her bouquet. And ranunculus." It was such a unique flower that even Petals & Leis had to special-order it onto the island. And Lisa had checked on that order at least three separate times in the past two months.

"Yes, those are supposed to be here two days prior," she said. "We got gorgeous orange and yellow and even some pale ones for all the centerpieces and the boutonnieres."

"That's right," Lisa said. "Only two days before? Will you have time to make everything? Regina has twenty-seven boutonnieres she needs, and she is not going to be happy if even one of them isn't right."

"We have everyone slated to work the two days prior to the wedding," Thea said. "We will be ready for the morning delivery." She smiled. "Have I ever let you down, Lisa?"

"Never." Lisa smiled at her friend. "Thanks so much, Thea."

Deirdre also added her thanks, and the video call ended. Deirdre sank into her chair and sighed. "Oh, my holy rose petals. That was the most stressful thing on the planet."

"I'm surprised Thea thought the gardenias were for Regina."

"Well, Gina and Jen do sound the same. Maybe I mumbled." Deirdre shrugged and looked at her screen again.

Lisa nodded, but she didn't think the mistake was Deirdre's. "Okay, flower emergency sorted. Wow, my heart is still beating a little too fast."

"Why do we schedule huge weddings on top of each other like this?" Deirdre asked. "I mean, the Chief of Police's daughter one weekend and the mayor's daughter the next?"

"And summer hasn't even started yet," Lisa said with a sigh. Which was honestly fine, because if Cal broke up with her, then she'd at least have dozens of tasks to keep her busy. But she didn't want wedding planning tasks occupying her every thought and all waking minutes.

She liked Cal, and she'd enjoyed the time she'd spent with him—and his daughter.

"Lisa?"

"Hmm?" She looked at Deirdre, realizing she'd disappeared inside her own mind.

"I asked if you'd eaten yet and wanted to run down to the taco railcar for lunch. Twenty minutes, and then we'll be back on these weddings."

Lisa thought of the salad sitting on her desk. Thought of the man who'd brought it. "Yeah," she said. "I can spare twenty minutes for tacos."

"Great." Deirdre grinned as she leaned forward and picked up her phone to call in their order. Then all they had to do was walk down the boardwalk, pick up their food, and eat it on the way back. Twenty minutes.

"How did dress shopping go last night?" she asked, and Lisa flinched. "Oh, not well, I see."

"No, the actually shopping part went great." The image of Sierra's glowing face as she wore that black dress floated through Lisa's mind. "It's just...I don't know." She didn't know how to articulate all she was feeling. She hadn't been able to last night once she'd made it home, and Cal's appearance and his blurted statement had only confused things more.

"She's your boyfriend's daughter, right?" Deirdre asked.

"Yeah," Lisa said, the misery in the single word not hard to hear, even to her own ears.

"What did she say?" Deirdre opened her drawer and pulled out her purse. "I'm buying the tacos. Let's go."

Lisa didn't answer as she followed her friend down

the hall. Deirdre paused at Sunny's desk, where Riley used to work, and another blast of missing her best friend hit her. She still hadn't been up to Riley's since checking on it once after the tsunami, and she vowed she'd go that night after she finished work.

Deirdre led them out into the sunshine too, and Lisa regretted not running back to her office to grab her sunglasses.

"Okay," Deirdre said. "So what did she say that has you all worried?"

"How do you know she said something?"

"I have a sixteen-year-old daughter myself," Deirdre said. "And trust me when I say, girls in their teens know exactly what to say to shatter your whole world."

Surprise moved through Lisa. "I didn't know you had a daughter."

"She lives with her father full-time now," Deirdre said, her voice cooling with every word. "I see her on weekends. Well, I'm supposed to. Our relationship is… difficult." She glanced at Lisa. "That's how I know this girl said something to you. How old is she?"

"Fourteen."

"Oh, the worst age." Deirdre smiled. "You don't have to tell me, but I might be able to help."

"She didn't even really say it to me." Lisa tried to remember exactly how the conversation had gone. "We'd bought the dress, which was really fun. She asked me to come in and help her with the sleeves, the zippers, all the buttons." A happiness moved through Lisa she didn't know she needed so desperately. "On the way home, she said something like, 'you know, you're not as fake as I thought you were.'"

"Oh, ouch."

"Yeah, so I found that out, and that she'd talked to her father about it, and he wasn't sure what to think." Her skin suddenly pimpled, as if she were cold. "He obviously puts a lot of stock into what his daughter thinks, because then he brought me a salad while I was on my conference call and said he needs to take our relationship slower."

Deirdre was kind enough to think about all Lisa had said, before she responded. "Maybe the two things aren't related."

"Yeah, maybe."

"How long have you been dating?"

"Since the company party."

"So only a few weeks."

"Right, and trust me, we haven't done anything or talked about anything that anyone would consider to be too fast." Except for Cal, obviously.

"Widower or divorced?" Deirdre asked.

"It's Cal Lewiston," she said. "You know him. He built Regina's altar."

"Oh, I didn't make that connection." Deirdre smiled at Lisa. "He's a great guy, but I still don't know if he's divorced or if his wife died."

"His wife died."

The conversation stalled as they arrived in the shade

at Manny's and picked up their food. "I will say this," Deirdre said. "Most men who are widowers do need to take things a little slow, especially if he hasn't dated before."

"Have you dated a widower?"

"Once," Deirdre said. "He wasn't ready, and our relationship didn't last long." She seemed wistful about it, and Lisa wondered what the story was behind those few words. But she simply bit into her fish taco, the lime and cilantro and spices making a party in her mouth.

She moaned, and Deirdre laughed. "Hey, at least we have fish tacos."

Lisa swallowed and said, "Yeah, and they're always ready and willing to be consumed quickly."

————

HOURS AND HOURS LATER, LISA PULLED UP TO RILEY'S house. The motion-sensor light came on, and everything looked fine on the outside. No burst pipes or signs of forced entry. Maybe Lisa had an overactive imagination. Maybe she just liked coming to this house where she'd spent so much time with her best friend.

She keyed her way into the house, and everything was just as normal inside as it had been out. She remembered when Sunshine and Marbles would run to greet her, how Riley would make their favorite tea after work sometimes—especially when one of them had just broken up with another boyfriend.

Trailing her fingers along Riley's counter, she went out the back door. The ocean glistened in the distance, and she'd always loved this view. "Miss you, Riles." She pulled out her phone and texted her friend.

All's well at the house. How's Malibu?

She wasn't sure if Riley was in California right now, as she traveled with her boyfriend's band, and Georgia Panic was one of the biggest bands in the world right now.

Not as fun as it would be if you were here.

For some reason, Riley's text made Lisa tear up, and she stared at her device, at a complete loss as to what to say. Riley had always been the one to help her through her relationship troubles, but she hadn't even told her about Cal.

And hey, I'm coming home in a couple of weeks, and I need a wedding planner...

Lisa shrieked and jabbed her finger on the call button. Riley answered with a laugh, and while Lisa felt like she was falling down, down, down into a dark pit, she was thrilled for her friend.

"I get to be the wedding planner, right?" she asked, bypassing the hello.

"Of course," Riley said. "But Evan hasn't asked yet. We just went ring shopping last night."

"Last *night?*" Lisa demanded. "And I'm just hearing about it now?"

"I know you're busy. The Gardner and the Keani weddings are right now."

"Riley," Lisa said, cocking her hip as if her friend was present with her. "You shouldn't know stuff like that."

"Yeah, well, I do," Riley said. "And not only that, but you've been keeping secrets yourself."

Lisa wanted to deny it, but she couldn't. "Who told you?"

"Charlotte."

"Yeah, well, it probably isn't going to work out. You know I like to keep my new dates on the down-low until I know if they're going somewhere."

"But Cal's great. I can't believe we never thought to ask him out before. Tell me how that happened."

Lisa thought of him sitting on that chaise beside the pool on the twenty-sixth floor, that drink in his hand almost gone....

She still hadn't gotten her dance—and she really, really wanted it.

Chapter Sixteen

Cal finished the construction at the Avenues as scheduled. He hadn't realized it, but Lisa had two big weddings she'd been working on, and the days passed, and one of the nuptials concluded.

He hadn't attended the wedding for Jennifer Gardner, though he was good friends with her father. He'd taken Sierra to the reception though, left a card with a little bit of money, and said hello to Wyatt Gardner, the Chief of Police.

Because of the public nature of his job, there had been people crammed into the open-air reception hall. Cal hadn't had much time to talk to Wyatt, which was probably okay. Cal didn't have much to say anyway, seemingly to anyone.

He hadn't said much to Lisa either. She'd texted him a little bit, and he'd responded when she did. But he hadn't seen her in the flesh for nine days now, and he wasn't even sure if they were still together or not. For all he knew, she could be going out with someone else every evening while he sat on his couch, dozing while he waited for Sierra to come home at night.

He spent more time thinking about and talking to Jo than he normally did, but he rationalized that he needed to, because their baby was about to go off to her first prom. He'd approved of the dress despite the sleeves being only on her upper arms and not actually over her shoulders. But the neckline was high, and it covered her back, and he'd decided shoulders showing were fine.

He literally couldn't fight about everything, and the phrase "pick your battles" had really started to mean something for him.

Cal stood at the sink, rinsing out the bowls he and his daughter had used for breakfast when she came down the hall, the tell-tale click of her heels preceding her. She appeared with every little piece in place, from her curled hair pinned to the top of her head, to the dangly earrings she'd borrowed from Hailey, who stood behind her.

"Wow," Cal said, still taking in the beautiful girl in front of him.

"I didn't go crazy with the makeup," Sierra said, and Cal nodded.

"No, you didn't. Let me see the shoes." He'd hated the red heels she'd first brought home, and they'd argued for an hour before she'd finally yelled, "Lisa said red heels! Why can't I just keep them?"

But with that pretty dress, and his slim daughter,

the heels made her look too old for him. A little bit too trashy. So he'd held his ground, and she'd taken the shoes back. Now she wore a pair of wedges with black straps across her feet and red ribbons that tied around her ankles. The splash of color was still there, but these shoes didn't say anything about undressing his daughter and doing adult things with her.

"Let me take your picture," he said. "Lisa will want to see." If Sierra had noticed that his girlfriend had stopped coming over, she hadn't said anything about it. Hailey moved out of the way, and Sierra posed so Cal could click a picture.

"You're so pretty," he said, gazing at her. "Your mother would've *loved* to see you like this."

"I know, Dad." Sierra came closer, and he hugged her. "Thank you for letting me go."

Cal didn't want to break down in front of anyone. He cleared his throat and stepped back. "Where's your dress, Hailey?"

"My mom is bringing it," she said. "She's supposed to be here any minute." She looked at her phone. "She better hurry up. The boys will be here in twenty minutes."

As if summoned by her daughter's displeasure, the doorbell rang. Hailey jumped toward it, and sure enough, her mother stood there with a garment bag. "I just picked it up. Let's see if it fits." She bustled into the house, throwing a look to where Cal stood with Sierra.

"Hey," Amie said. "Wow, Sierra, look at you." She beamed from ear to ear. "Can we…?"

"Yep, use my room," Sierra said, and Amie went down the hall with Hailey.

Cal turned back to load the dishes in the dishwasher.

"So, did you break up with Lisa?" Sierra asked.

He dropped the two bowls, both of them clattering onto the lower rack. Straightening, he looked at his daughter. "Honestly? I don't know."

"You don't know if you broke up?" Sierra rolled her eyes. "Dad, that's not usually how things work."

"Well, I'm not fourteen," he said, a note of disgust in his voice. "I mean, you were with Travis one day, and then the next, you went to the outdoor cinema with Justin." He set the bowls in the rack properly and looked at his daughter again. "Right?"

"Yeah, but I am fourteen," she said. "And…you liked Lisa."

He still did, but he didn't know how to explain anything to Sierra. He didn't understand so many things himself. "I told her I wanted to move a little slower," he said. "So we've been texting."

"Dad, that's backward, not slower."

"Hey, I see some of the things boys text you. Trust me, they're not thinking slow when they say they want to get you alone behind the bleachers."

Sierra rolled her eyes, but her texts kept Cal up at night. "Yeah, but those guys are scumbags," she said. "You're a *nice* guy, Dad."

"So what do nice guys text?" he asked.

"They ask to sit by me at lunch," Sierra said. "Or to ride our bikes up to the waterfall. That kind of stuff."

"Sit by you at lunch." He narrowed his eyes at her. "And who have you been sitting by?"

"Mikel," she said with a smile. "And Dad, he's nice too."

Cal couldn't respond, because Hailey came down the hall in her dress, and Sierra started shrieking. Amie made the two girls pose in front of the window so the natural light fell onto their faces. She told them how wonderful they were, and kept tucking stray strands of hair back where they belonged.

She said, "Now, listen, ladies. If any of these boys—"

"Mom," Hailey said, darting a glance at Cal.

"Oh, I want to hear this," he said. "Go on."

"You're fourteen years old," Amie said. "Too young for sex. Don't go off alone with your date. You may think he's a nice guy, but he's still a hormonal, fourteen-year-old boy."

Cal was in awe of how Amie could lecture, and he wished he'd taken a video of her.

"Stay together," she said. "Watch out for each other. You have a phone. Use it if you need to. We will come get you, no matter what, no matter where, no questions asked. Okay?" She looked at Hailey and then Sierra, who both nodded.

Amie looked at Cal. "Any last words? The boys will be here any second."

"What she said," Cal said, and Sierra giggled. "And I will be the bad guy," he said. "If you don't want to do something and don't know how to say no, call or text me, and *I'll* say no."

"Oh, good one," Amie said with a smile. "What's our safe word tonight?"

The girls looked at each other, and Cal looked at Amy. "I just usually ask Sierra—is this something you want to do? And she can say yes or no."

"That works," Amie said as the doorbell rang. "Oh, they're here. I get as many pictures as I want. No arguing." She gathered both girls into a hug. "You're going to have so much fun."

Cal marveled at how easily Amie interacted with and seemed to relate to Sierra and Hailey. And he was totally stealing the idea of telling his daughter what he wanted and that she couldn't argue.

"I get to answer the door," he said, hurrying to step in front of Sierra. "And you can't get mad at me for asking a couple of questions."

"Dad," she said, but she didn't try to stop him. He walked over to the door and opened it to find two young men standing on his doorstep. A big SUV sat in his driveway, with a man behind the wheel and a woman in the passenger seat. The Palau's. Cal raised his hand to wave to them, and then looked at the teenagers on his porch.

"Gentlemen," he said. "What are your plans for tonight?"

"Uh, dinner," Mikel said, his eyes wide and full of anxiety. "And then we're going to the school."

"What time will my daughter be home?" he asked.

"Midnight."

"Your parents are driving the whole night?"

"Dad," Sierra hissed behind him, and Mikel nodded.

"You don't drink, do you?"

"Dad," Sierra said louder now.

"No, sir," Mikel said.

"What about you?" Cal looked at the other boy, whom he didn't know.

"No, sir."

"Our daughters will be safe with you?"

"Yes, sir," they said together.

"All right." He stepped back. "You better come in. Mrs. Fixdale wants a lot of pictures." The two boys stepped past him and into his home, and Cal tried not to enjoy his fatherly role quite so much.

Amie did take a lot of pictures, and then they sent Hailey and Sierra out the door with their dates.

Cal leaned against the counter and sighed, and Amie collapsed into a chair at his kitchen table. "That was terrible," he said.

"And it's only the beginning," Amie said.

They both started laughing, and she said, "I'll send you some of these," as she scrolled through her phone.

"That would be great," he said. "Do you want some coffee?" He didn't normally drink coffee in the evenings, and he was certainly already keyed up from the events that had just happened. But he knew his adrenaline would crash, and he had to stay up until midnight tonight to make sure everything with Sierra was okay.

"Yes, coffee would be lovely," Amie said, smiling at him.

Cal turned to start making the brew when his doorbell rang again. He glanced at Amie, but of course, she didn't know who it was. They moved toward the door together, and she said, "Watch, one of those boys is freaking out. I knew fourteen was too young for the prom."

Cal chuckled and opened the door, expecting a lanky teenage boy.

He got Lisa. His gorgeous, blonde-haired goddess —Lisa.

Sucking in a breath, he tried to speak at the same time, and the result was a squeak.

"Hey," she said, and then her eyes moved to Amie. "Oh, I'm sorry. I didn't know...." She tucked her hair behind her ear and looked back at Cal, clear accusations in her eyes. "Did I miss Sierra? I wanted to wish her luck tonight."

"The girls just left," Amie said. "Cal was just putting on coffee."

"Oh, was he?" Lisa glared at him now. "That's funny, because Cal doesn't drink coffee in the evenings." She folded her arms, obviously waiting for him to say something.

Problem was, he had no idea what to say.

Chapter Seventeen

L isa could not believe the man in front of her. She had not pegged him for a cheater. At all. Of course, she also hadn't expected his "slower" to mean "I'm going to completely disappear and only text you when you text me first."

So she was learning all kinds of things about the man.

"I should go," Amie said. "Call me if you hear anything from the girls." She slipped out of the house and past Lisa as if Lisa were made of smoke.

"Who was that?" she asked as a car started up behind her.

"Amie," he said. "Hailey's mom." He stepped back, fear still in his eyes. "Do you want coffee?"

"No," she said, confusion starting to creep through her anger. "Are you seeing her?"

"Of course not. She's married with three kids."

"And that matters how?" Lisa asked. "People have affairs all the time."

"Oh, wow," Cal said, settling his weight on his back foot. "Do you really think I'd do that?"

"Did you really think I was fake when your daughter called me that?" Lisa hadn't come here to fight with him. She'd come to give Sierra a big hug, and she'd been hoping she could crash with Cal on the couch for a few hours. Talk to him. Find out if ten days apart was slow enough. She'd pulled into his driveway dying to kiss him.

Now she just wanted to run away.

Cal shook his head, but Lisa didn't know if it was in disbelief or if he was saying no. The anger deflated from her, physically making her shoulders slump.

"Look, I'm sorry," she said. "That caught me off-guard." She turned and took a few steps. "I just wanted to see Sierra."

"Wait," he said, but she'd already started down the steps. Her wedged shoes didn't allow her to stop once she got going downhill, so she didn't stop until she reached the sidewalk.

She turned back to him, but he said nothing. "I hope she has fun, Cal. Call me when you're really ready to be dating again." The words may have come out a little sharp, but she couldn't really tell right now. She hurried to her car and got behind the wheel.

For some reason, being locked in the car offered some measure of safety, though she could still see Cal standing at the top of his porch through her window. She flipped the car in reverse and got out of his driveway. Down the road.

Relief spread through her, helping her muscles release. Her fingers still gripped the steering wheel too tightly, and she didn't make the turn she needed to in order to get back to her house.

She drove around the island, unsure of her final destination, only that she didn't want to go home alone.

She found herself at Riley's house, though that wasn't much better than her own place. *But Cal won't be able to show up*, she thought, and she actually liked the layer of protection between her and him at Riley's.

After flipping on all the lights in the house and making sure she was locked in and alone, Lisa did brew some coffee. Her thoughts rotated, never landing on any one thread.

When she finally got the courage to look at her phone, she'd missed a call from Cal and had five text messages from him as well.

I have never thought you were fake, he'd said.

I'll tell Sierra you stopped by.

Amie and I have never seen each other. I would never participate in a relationship like that.

So you won't answer your phone.

Did we just break up?

Lisa just stared at the words as the scent of coffee filled the house. Then she set the phone face-down on the counter and poured herself a cup, hoping Riley had left sugar in the house. She used to know where it was, and when she opened the cupboard next to the stove, she found the cute little bowl with plenty of sugar in it.

No cream, but at least Lisa didn't have to drink her coffee black and bitter.

She didn't want to break up with Cal, but she feared he wanted a much different relationship than she did. She'd be lying if she said she hadn't been hoping to talk to him about that tonight too.

Her stomach growled, and Lisa knew drinking coffee while she was hungry would leave her with an unpleasant buzz. She picked up her phone again, ignoring the texts this time, and navigating to the food delivery app. Once she had some excellent Thai food on its way to Riley's house, she finally took her first sip of coffee.

She sat on the back porch in the skirt she'd worn to work that day, and she watched the sun sink into the ocean. The minutes seemed to slip away as easily as breathing, and then drag.

Her food arrived, and she ate her way through noodles and chicken and soup before feeling like herself again.

Only then did she face her phone. Cal would be awake until Sierra came home from the prom, so she could call him. Tell him…what, exactly?

She dialed his number anyway, because she'd gone to his house to see him and talk. They could at least do one of those things.

"Lisa," he said, panicked and relieved at the same time.

Lisa didn't know what to say. The first thing that came to her mind also came out of her mouth. "Yes, I think we should break up."

Silence met her ears, and she waited for Cal to say something.

"All right," he said in that sexy voice of his.

"That's it?" Sure, they'd only been dating for a few weeks, but she'd really liked him. And she'd thought he liked her. A hot knife sliced right down the middle of her body, separating her left half from her right. She took quick gulps of air, wondering how she'd gotten to this point *again*.

"I'm not a cheater."

"I know that," she said.

He sighed, a very audible form of his frustration. "But you did say something that I think is right." He cleared his throat, and she imagined what his face would look like as anxious as he was. Adorable. Handsome. Vulnerable. All things Lisa loved in a man.

"I don't think I'm quite ready to date again."

Lisa started nodding, though she didn't have anyone to see her. "Yeah, I figured when you said we needed to slow down after only three weeks of seeing each other a few times."

Cal didn't say anything, so she didn't know what he was thinking or feeling. "I'm sorry," he said. "I thought I was ready."

"Like I said, call me when you are." Lisa didn't really hear what he said after that, and when he said, "Thanks,

Lisa," she pressed her eyes closed so she wouldn't have tear tracks on her face.

The call ended, and Lisa wanted to throw her phone through the nearest window. Before she could, the device buzzed, and she couldn't help looking down at it.

Clean up party, ten a.m. Charlotte had texted. *Starting with brunch at my place. Bring your SOs.*

Smiley faces and thumbs up emojis started flying in, and Lisa put her head in her hands and cried.

Brunch with her significant other. What would that be like?

She cried because she feared she'd never have a significant other that lasted more than a month or two. She cried because she'd go alone and pretend to be happy for everyone while she was dying a slow death inside. She cried because she missed Cal fiercely.

And she cried because now she had to start all over again. Twenty-six dates until she found someone who might be able to stand being with her for longer than a few weeks.

————

LISA LEFT HER PHONE IN HER OFFICE, KNOWING FULL-well that she'd have a zillion messages by the time she got back to it. She didn't care.

Brunch started at ten, and that meant everyone wouldn't get to Your Tidal Forever until at least noon.

Lisa walked in at nine-thirty, wearing the same clothes she'd been wearing to the wedding yesterday afternoon.

She changed into a pair of shorts and a T-shirt—emergency clothing she kept in her office—and got to work undressing the trellises, winding up the tea lights, and putting everything in its correctly labeled box.

The work was easy and slow and methodical. Exactly what she needed for the morning after a break-up. She didn't want to see anyone, as then they'd realize her puffy eyes meant she'd spent a long time crying last night.

And she was simply too old to cry over a relationship that had barely lasted a month.

She did miss Cal though, and he had been different than the other men she'd dated. She was just getting Sierra to open up to her, and regret lanced through her because she hadn't been able to see the teen in her prom dress, all made up and ready for the dance.

At noon, Lisa collected her clothes and phone from her office and slipped outside. She made it out of the parking lot without seeing anyone from the company, and she drove through a burger joint so she'd have something to eat.

When she finally pulled into her own driveway, she was ready to be home.

Her afternoon in sweats, with a pint of ice cream and a chick flick, vanished before her eyes when she saw a figure rise from one of the chairs she kept on her front porch. A moment later, Sierra leaned over the railing.

Lisa's pulse went from zero to sixty in less than a

single breath. The teenager didn't smile or seem all that thrilled to see Lisa, but she also wasn't flying down the steps in a panic. Lisa got out of the car and called, "Hey. What are you doing here? How was the prom?"

That got Sierra to smile, and she ducked her head. So the prom had been great.

"It was fun," Sierra said, the same type of answer Lisa used to give her mom when she didn't want to expound on the details. "My dad said you came by and just missed me."

"Yeah," Lisa said, arriving on the porch too. "I tried to get away from the wedding as fast as I could. We were cleaning up this morning." She gestured to the chairs, and they sat down. "You haven't been here long, have you?"

"Only an hour or so."

Lisa looked at Sierra, not wanting to beat around the bush with her. "An hour? What's going on?"

"My dad is in a bad way," she said.

"Excuse me?" Lisa asked. She smiled at Sierra. "I'm old. Translate for me."

"He's miserable," she said, giggling. "Not that that's funny." She shook her head and sobered. "He was banging pans around this morning, and he burnt the coffee, and then he took the whole coffeemaker out to the trashcan and declared he was giving up the stuff."

"But coffee in his love language," Lisa said.

"Yeah, that's how I knew something was wrong,"

Sierra said. "And he is not nice when he's not caffeinated, let me tell you."

Lisa managed a quick smile. "We broke up."

"I heard." Sierra tucked her hair behind her ear. "Why?"

Once again, Lisa wanted to be truthful with the girl. "Honestly?"

"Yeah, I don't need things sugar-coated."

"He's not ready," Lisa said. "He'll always love your mother, I get that. But he is just not ready for another real, serious, loving relationship right now." The words stung even as she said them, because they were true.

"He wants to be," Sierra said.

"There's a difference between wanting something and actually being able to do it," Lisa said gently. She drew in a deep breath. "Now, do you have any pictures from last night? I want to see your hair and your makeup and the whole ensemble."

Sierra just watched her for a minute, finally smiling.

"What?" Lisa asked.

"I think you actually do want to see the pictures."

"Of course I do," Lisa said, sitting back in her chair.

"I was wrong about you, Lisa," Sierra said. "You aren't fake, and you're actually really nice."

Every muscle tightened and then relaxed. "Thank you."

"Maybe my dad wasn't the only one not ready for him to move on," Sierra said. "I'm sorry I wasn't that nice to you."

Affection for this young woman touched Lisa's heart, and she reached over and gripped Sierra's hand. "It's okay. All is forgiven."

Sierra gave another smile tinged with sadness and swiped on her phone. "Okay, so Hailey's mom took these. I think we look pretty good." She handed the phone to Lisa, who stared at the beauty in front of her.

"Oh, Sierra," she sighed. "These are more than pretty good. You're beautiful." She cast a quick look at her. "I wish I had made it on time."

"Next time," Sierra said, and Lisa actually believed the teen wanted her to be involved next time she had a big dance to attend.

"Yeah," Lisa said, knowing it would never happen. "Next time."

Chapter Eighteen

C al watched Sierra throw a few snacks together and call it a lunch. He hadn't gotten up and showered, the way he usually did. "Grandma will be here after school."

His break-up with Lisa had happened on Saturday night, and he'd barely made it through Sunday without burning his house to the ground. So cooking was out. So was socializing. And parenting. And apparently, working.

"You've told me four times," Sierra said.

"I'll be back on Thursday."

"Yep," she said. "Going around to Lightning Point, so you're not that far away. Fishing boat. Hut in the rain forest. Got it." She flashed him a smile that still let him know she was frustrated with him.

He was frustrated with himself too. "Okay." He pressed a kiss to her forehead and added, "Be safe. Love you."

"Love you too, Dad." Sierra hitched her backpack over her shoulder and hesitated.

"What?" he asked.

She opened her mouth to say something, and then shook her head. "Nothing. See you Thursday."

Before he could call her back, she walked out the door, leaving Cal in the house alone. He actually loved being alone, and he was practically running away from his life for a few days. To fish alone. Make solo meals. Sleep alone. Live in the rainforest alone.

But before all of that, he needed to shower, pack, and attend a grief meeting. He'd attended the support group for several months after Jo's death, but he hadn't been to a meeting in a while.

Too long.

He hadn't even been sure where they were meeting anymore, but he'd looked it up online, and they had a meeting at noon today. He could attend, drive around the island to Lightning Point, and try to find some peace before returning on Thursday.

When he walked into the meeting, his nerves struck like lightning. When he'd been coming before, he knew all of the faces in the group. Now, he only recognized one.

Chief of Police, Wyatt Gardner.

Surprise moved through Cal, because Wyatt's wife had died years ago too. Their eyes met, and Wyatt stood up. Cal moved in his direction and shook the Chief's hand. "Hey," he said, accepting the quick embrace and pat on the back. "You're still coming to these?"

"It's good to see you here," Wyatt said. "I don't know anyone here."

"So you haven't been coming."

"It's my second meeting in a long time," he said.

Cal wanted to ask him why he'd come back, but his own reason was personal, and he didn't feel like sharing it.

"My first," Cal said.

"Yeah," the Chief said, clearing his throat. "I want to ask out this woman, but…." He shrugged. "I don't know. I feel like maybe I still need some closure."

Cal looked at Wyatt. "I just broke up with my girl-friend. Well, she broke up with me." The words actually scraped his throat. "She said I wasn't ready to be dating, and well…." He shrugged too. "She's right."

"But you want to be ready," Wyatt said.

"Here I am." Cal flashed his old friend a smile, glad he was still able to do so. When he'd first started coming to these grief meetings, he'd barely been able to sit in the chair and focus. Wyatt Gardner had been there, in the corner seat in the last row. He was Cal's age, and he'd lost his wife to the same cancer that had taken Jo.

Cal had felt in Wyatt a kindred spirit from the moment he'd sat next to him, barely able to say his own name and who he was grieving.

"Jen's married now," Wyatt said, sighing. "The house is empty without her there."

"I'm sorry," Cal said, though he should be saying congratulations. But he would be in the same position as Wyatt in just a few short years.

"It's a good thing," Wyatt said, smiling. "But seeing my daughter so excited to spend her life with Aaron, watching her at the ceremony…." He shrugged in a very vulnerable way, and Cal saw beneath the tough police exterior Wyatt usually kept in place. "I decided I could at least try to find someone else to spend the rest of my life with. I mean, I'm only forty-six."

"I'll be forty in January," Cal said.

"Plenty of time," Wyatt said. "Did you like the girl-friend?" He looked at Cal with questions in his eyes.

"I…yeah," Cal said, wishing the simple words didn't make his heart come to a full stop. When it started beating again, it actually thumped in his throat. He flashed another smile at his friend, glad when someone stood up and said it was time to begin the meeting.

Lisa had said to call him when he was ready to date again, and he really wanted to be ready. So he sat in the meeting, completely present. He listened, and his heart hurt for those whose loved ones had passed away so recently.

He supposed it didn't matter how much time had passed since a death, as his own pain indicated. As Wyatt's presence next to him testified.

At one grief meeting years ago, Cal had learned that he didn't need to forget about Jo. He could love her forever. He could think about her and miss her and talk to her, and that was normal. Expected, even.

But he'd forgotten that his life didn't have to be wrapped up in her death. As he looked around at the other people in the meeting, he saw them in different stages of grief. Some so new and so fresh to the pain of loss. Some working their way through it. Some on the outer cusp, like him and Wyatt.

But he wasn't completely free from it, and he wasn't sure he ever would be. Peace descended on him, almost like Jo coming to sit beside him. He actually looked to the seat next to him, expecting her to be there.

Of course she wasn't, but he could hear her voice for those few brief moments when she'd made him promise to find someone else to share his life with.

Meet someone new, Cal. Mingle.

His emotions choked him, and he hurried to cross his arms, hoping that physical act would contain the emotional turmoil. Wyatt glanced over at him, and Cal managed a shaky smile. Wyatt patted Cal's shoulder, and Cal appreciated their friendship so much.

The meeting ended, and Cal stood with several others. His first instinct was to rush out the door. His bags were packed, the truck fully gassed up. He needed a few days to find his center again, figure out where he was going, and how he wanted to get there. Who he wanted to be with on the journey and at the destination.

Mingle.

He stayed and chatted with the Chief, learned his

daughter was moving completely off-island, and that Wyatt was ready to be out of the public spotlight. They'd migrated over to the refreshment table, and Cal introduced himself to a younger man named Stephen Morgan.

His longer hair and dark circles under his eyes indicated that his loss had been quite recently. "Who is your loved one?"

Stephen looked at him. "You said *is*. Not was." His eyes started to water, and Cal wanted to grab the man in a tight hug and tell him everything would be okay. But he'd never liked it when people told him that.

"Of course," Cal said, glancing at Wyatt. He really wasn't good at this kind of emotional stuff. "Your loved one *is* still with you. You don't forget about them because they're gone physically. They don't just disappear from our lives."

"Your wife?" Wyatt asked.

Stephen nodded, his chin shaking. "Just a few weeks ago."

"Any kids?"

"No, thank goodness."

Cal almost flinched, and something must've shown on his face, because horror crossed Stephen's. "I'm sorry. You have kids."

"We both do," Wyatt said easily. "Daughters." He sounded so proud of that fact, and Cal suddenly was proud to be Sierra's father. He'd done the best he could with raising her, and in that moment, he knew he'd done enough so far. He'd keep checking on the clothes she wore, and insisting he know who she spent her time with. He'd keep asking Jo for help, and he'd keep doing the very best he could.

CAL SAT ON THE FRONT PORCH OF THE TINY CABIN HE owned in the middle of the rainforest. He and Jo had bought the place in the first year of their marriage, and they'd kept it up so they could enjoy vacations to this side of the island. The beach was a short half-mile walk through the trees and seemed to open up to the sprawling ocean in an instant.

He loved the peace here. The way the birds chirped in the morning. The sense of heavy humidity in the air. He'd planned to get one of his father's fishing boats out of the storage shed and hit the water the moment he arrived, but he'd been rocking on the porch for a couple of hours now.

He was only thirty-nine, but he felt decades older. At least right now. He didn't want to go fishing. He was perfectly happy to sit here and think.

His mind wandered through Jo, Sierra, the men on his crew, and finally to Lisa. He appreciated the things and people he had in his life. He loved the business he'd been able to build for himself. He loved his crew, his daughter.

Everything surrounding those parts of his life were crystal clear.

When he got to Lisa, everything became a bit muddied.

"Where do I start?" he asked the palm trees surrounding him. He tipped his head back and closed his eyes.

It was always best to start at the beginning, and his memory cleared enough to remember the pretty blonde who'd approached him at the pool party on the twenty-sixth floor of the Sweet Breeze Resort and Spa.

She'd finished his drink, which he found odd but also extremely attractive.

She'd asked him to dance—something they still hadn't done.

Something he still really wanted to do—and that told him so much. That desire told him he was willing to mingle. Willing to do whatever it took to get on the same path with Lisa.

He could only hope that by the time he found his way to that path, that she would be still available and willing to dance with him.

Chapter Nineteen

Lisa squealed as she saw Riley's red hair bobbing through the crowd. Of course, she was easy to find because her rockstar boyfriend was a head taller than everyone, wore dark sunglasses, and had a security detail clearing a path for them.

"Riley," she called, and her friend broke toward her. Lisa laughed at the same time she cried a little bit, hugging her best friend.

Summer had fully arrived on the island, and tourists streamed past them at the airport. "Oh, don't cry," Riley said, wiping her own eyes. "We'll be here for a month, and it's going to be so great."

"Yeah, except I still have to go to work every day," Lisa said. Evan Garfield approached, and Lisa shook his hand. "Let's get to the office and get our meeting over with. I'm just so happy for you two." Her voice broke, and she ducked her head away from the newly engaged couple whose wedding she was going to plan.

Just six short months until Riley and Evan's beach wedding, and Lisa was determined to make sure every single detail was absolutely correct.

She hugged them both, and they left the airport together. She wanted to lounge by a pool with someone bringing her a cold drink as she told Riley about her relationship with Cal. Of course, that had been over for almost six weeks now, but Lisa couldn't stop thinking about him. She hadn't been out with anyone new, and she didn't even want to see someone else.

She wasn't sure how or when Cal had reached right into her chest and stolen her heart. She wasn't sure if she loved him or not. She knew how to set an alarm and get up on time. She knew how to feed her dog, make coffee, and drive to work. She knew how to order pretty papers and pick out the perfectly pink petals for a ceremony.

Her friendship with Deirdre had broadened, and she'd actually been very helpful in understanding a little bit more about Cal and what he was going through.

Riley linked her arm through Lisa's, and her loneliness these past few weeks faded a little. Riley had a ton of stories about the places she'd been, the things she'd been doing for Georgia Panic, and she somehow knew Lisa didn't want to talk.

So Riley did, all the way to Your Tidal Forever. The reunion there was epic, as Lisa had made sure everyone knew Riley and her new fiancé would be coming in.

Sunny had ordered sandwiches and cake, and several of their distributors and contractors had come in.

One of those contractors would've been Cal Lewiston, and Lisa had been sure to put his invite on Deirdre's list so she wouldn't have to contact him. Not that she expected him to show up. Sure, he knew Riley, but they weren't the best of friends.

Cal had other jobs, and even when he had built something for Your Tidal Forever over the past six weeks, he hadn't interacted with Lisa.

She had kept in touch with Sierra, and whether Cal knew or not, Lisa wasn't sure. She'd asked Sierra to tell her father, make sure their communication was okay, but she'd never followed up with the teenager.

She also knew Cal checked his daughter's phone, so unless Sierra was deleting their text string, Cal would know about the conversations whether Sierra told him explicitly or not.

The lobby of Your Tidal Forever had been decorated with white and yellow balloons, streamers, and all of the refreshments. When Lisa entered, everyone started cheering, and Riley stood there and cried until Charlotte rushed over to her.

"You guys are too much," she said.

"Oh, you would've done this for any of us coming back," Shannon said, and Lisa had to agree. Riley was the ultimate queen in keeping details and appointments and making sure everyone who walked through the door felt like royalty.

She mingled about, and Lisa stepped over to the refreshment table to get herself a piece of cake. This party wasn't unlike the spring company party from a few months ago, and Lisa flashed back to the feeling of being an outsider she'd felt among that crowd by the pool.

Maybe there was someone else here she could get to know better. Make a new friend. Maybe another of their contractors was single and looking for a date.

She found a spot halfway behind Sunny's desk, a safe spot she could watch the party as she sipped her soda. The festivities wouldn't last much longer, and then she'd steal Evan and Riley away from their friends. Business would go back to normal at Your Tidal Forever, and Lisa would take notes with Charlotte and Sunny, detailing everything Riley wanted for her own wedding.

A stab of jealousy hit her heart, no matter how hard she pushed against it. She loved Riley and had always wanted her to find a man like Evan. Problem was, she wanted her own version of Evan Garfield too. A man who was her own personal rockstar.

Her phone buzzed against her leg, and she pulled it out of her pocket to check it. It was the height of the summer wedding season after all, and she did have four upcoming weddings before September.

But the message wasn't from a bride. She sucked in a breath as she read Cal's message—*do you want to dance with me?*—and immediately looked up to find him.

No one was dancing here the way they had been at the pool, but Lisa's pulse didn't care about that.

She also couldn't find Cal, and then suddenly someone moved, and there he stood. Only a few feet away, he took two steps and took her drink and her phone from her.

He finished her soda and set the plastic cup, along with her phone, on the desk beside her. "So?" he asked. "Did you get my text?"

Cal had just gotten his hair cut. His sexy beard was neatly trimmed, and all Lisa could do was drown in the depths of his dark blue eyes.

He inched closer to her, completely cutting off her view of the rest of the party. "I've been attending my grief meetings again," he said, his voice quiet enough to make Lisa lean forward to hear him. "I'm feeling so much better, and I'm hoping you'll be available for dinner tonight."

"Tonight?" Lisa asked, surprised her voice worked at all. Her mind whirred through her schedule, and she was pretty sure she was supposed to hang out with Riley that night.

"Let me know, okay?" Cal backed up a step and then another, expanding her world again. He returned to her and leaned down, pressing his lips to her cheek. "I hope you can make it," he whispered, his voice delicious and soft, for her ears only.

She stayed against the desk as he fell back again, and when he turned and left, her eyes landed on Riley's. Her friend abandoned the conversation she'd been having with Hope and came straight toward Lisa.

Lisa looked at the cup on the desk and back to Riley. "Who was that?" she said in half a hiss and half of a normal voice.

"Cal Lewiston," Lisa said, still a little shocked at how different he'd seemed. More confident. More sure of himself and sure of what he wanted. More…ready.

She smiled at Riley, and added, "Okay, look, I know we were planning dinner tonight, but he just asked me out, and I didn't tell you, but I dated him a little bit ago, and I really like him." Lisa knew she was talking too fast, but Riley would be able to keep up. Her eyes sparkled, and she nodded.

"You go right ahead," Riley said. "I'll be here for a month, and there will be plenty of time for you to tell me all about him." She glanced over her shoulder as if Cal would still be standing there, but Lisa knew he wasn't. "Because, wow."

"It's Cal," Lisa said, a burst of laughter coming out of her mouth next. "We've worked with him for years."

"Sometimes the stars just need to align," Riley said. "I can't wait to hear about it."

Lisa couldn't wait to tell her. But at the moment, she also couldn't wait to see Cal again. She grabbed her phone and sent him a quick text.

Yes.

"Okay, let's go plan your wedding," she said to Riley, another squeal coming out of her mouth. This time, it was for Riley—and for her date with Cal that night.

Chapter Twenty

C al paced from the front door to the kitchen table, where Sierra bent over to light the last candle. "Dad," she said. "You have to chill."

"What if this doesn't work?" He rubbed his hands together, so nervous. Lisa had only sent him one single word since this morning when he'd crashed her party at Your Tidal Forever.

Yes.

As words go, Cal really liked that one. He'd texted back to let her know dinner would be at his house at seven.

And it was seven-oh-five.

The back door opened, and he nearly jumped out of his skin. "Sea, are you almost ready?"

Mikel stood there, and Cal barely blinked at him. He was a nice kid, and Cal actually liked him. He came over to the house and watched movies, made Sierra laugh, and had helped her with her final computer project at the end of the year. Now that summer had arrived, Mikel and Sierra went to the beach with friends, and he'd just turned fifteen, so his father was teaching him how to drive.

As far as boys Cal would like his daughter hanging out with, Mikel was one of the better ones.

But he just wanted the doorbell to ring and Lisa to be standing on the porch.

"Not for a few minutes," she said. "You can come in. My dad's girlfriend isn't here yet."

"She's not my girlfriend," Cal said automatically.

"Okay, the woman he wants to be his girlfriend isn't here yet." She rolled her eyes at Cal, but he barely noticed. The collar on this shirt was too tight, and he reached up to touch the buttons there. The top two were already undone, and Sierra moved over in front of him.

She swatted his hands away from his neck. "Dad, the shirt is awesome."

"I don't like shirts like this," he said.

"But you look great, and the idea is to look great tonight. Right?" She put both hands on his shoulders and looked right into his eyes. "Calm down. It's Lisa."

He nodded. "Right. Lisa." He'd asked for Sierra's input over the past week to help him put together a plan to get Lisa back. He'd told her, "I'm ready, Sea. I'm really ready, and I don't really want to mingle like Mom said. I like Lisa—I *really* like Lisa—and I want to see if our relationship can turn into love."

Sierra had hugged him, and then she'd started giving him all kinds of advice. What to wear. What to do. What to eat. What to say.

All of it felt stirred up into one big pot of soup inside his mind.

The doorbell rang, and he spun toward the front door.

"Go," Sierra said, and Cal practically sprinted down the hall and into the safety of his bedroom. The plan was to have Sierra open the door. She'd been talking to Lisa over the course of the last six weeks, as Cal had discovered when he'd performed his routine checks of her phone. At first, he'd been angry. Then he'd realized that he couldn't take Lisa away from Sierra, and he'd kept working on himself.

He heard feminine voices coming from the front of the house, and he counted to five, as per his daughter's instructions. He pulled on the bottom of that blasted blue shirt, covered with tiny yellow pineapples, and headed down the hall.

Rounding the corner, he paused, because Lisa had pulled out all the stops. Her hair fell in beautiful waves over her shoulders, a blonde waterfall he wanted to run his fingers through. She wore something different than what she'd had on at Your Tidal Forever this morning, and he sure did like the little black dress, the blue ballet flats, and the way she smiled at him.

He returned the smile, still nervous but not so out of his head that he couldn't walk toward her. He took her easily into his arms, and said, "Hey. It's so great to see you. Thanks for coming."

Stepping back, he cleared his throat. "My daughter made me wear this shirt."

Lisa giggled and looked at Sierra, who was smiling at her with shining eyes.

"This is my boyfriend, Mikel," she said, pulling the kid toward her. "I went to the prom with him too."

"Oh, you're the prom date." Lisa scanned him from head to toe and looked at Sierra. "He's cute, Sea."

"Right?" The girls laughed, and then Sierra put her hand in Mikel's and said, "We're going, Dad."

"Okay," he said, almost absently. "Call me if you're not going to be at Mikel's."

"Yep."

"Be safe," he said, just like he always did. "Love you."

"Love you too." The back door closed, and he was alone with Lisa, something he'd been dreaming about for a while.

He blinked and backed up a step. "Okay, so come sit over here. Sierra ordered our food for tonight, and she helped me get the table set and everything."

"She's a good girl," Lisa said, and Cal could only agree.

"I had this whole speech memorized," he said. "But I've sort of forgotten it." He chuckled, the sound full of nerves. He pulled open the oven and removed the Hawaiian barbecue pork Sierra said was all the rage.

"Is that pork from Kiki's?" she asked.

"Yes," he said. "And if you'll sit down, I'll serve you up a plate." He hurried to pull her chair out for her, and she looked up at him as she sat. Cal threw everything out the window and knelt down at her side.

"I missed you," he said. "So much. And I'm ready, Lisa. When Jo was dying, she told me to get out there and meet someone else. Mingle." He shook his head, his nerves releasing now that he was talking. "I'm not sure if you remember much about me, but I'm not a mingler."

"No, I wouldn't classify you that way," she said with a smile.

"You changed my life when you came over to me and finished my drink at that party." Cal could still see the situation clearly in his head, as if she'd just done it yesterday. "And I want to dance with you. I want to learn everything I can about you, and I want to see if we can hire someone at your firm to plan our wedding. I'll build our altar—anything you want."

He pulled back on his thoughts, because he'd gotten way too far ahead of himself. Lisa's eyes glittered with tears, and Cal smiled at her.

"I don't know if I'm in love with you," he said. "But I want to find out." There. That was the end of the speech. He gazed at her, waiting for her to say something.

She smiled, the movement shaky, and she leaned toward him. "I want to find out too."

He took her face in both of his hands and kissed her, and Lisa kissed him right back. He felt alive in a way he hadn't in so long, and he couldn't wait to tell her about everything he'd been working on these past six weeks.

"Will you dance with me?" he whispered.

She nodded, and he straightened and took her into his arms. She fit right inside the circle of his arms, smelling of roses and oranges, and he pressed his cheek right against hers as he held her close.

True happiness flowed over him, and he closed his eyes and thought, *Thank you, Jo*, as he and Lisa danced to music only they could hear.

An hour later, he sat with Lisa on the couch, their dinner delicious, but now gone. "So I've been getting back to my roots," he said. "Visiting my parents. Learning how to make fishing boats from my father. Attending grief meeting every week."

"Wow," she said. She'd been a very good listener as he detailed for her his efforts. "Cal, I didn't mean—I feel a little guilty. Like you weren't good enough for me before."

"Don't feel like that," he said. "That's not true at all. It wasn't a self-confidence issue."

She nodded and studied her hands. "Okay."

"I loved my wife," he said. "Very much. We had a lot of time together at the end, and I know she wanted me to move on. Still took me a long time, and I probably wouldn't be where I am without you coming over and asking me to dance."

He reached over and gently lifted her chin, so she'd look at him. "So thank you, Lisa." He touched his lips to hers. "Now, do you want to go to a grief meeting with me? They're every Monday at noon."

"Oh," she said, clearly surprised. "I don't know. Do I need to—do people like me go?"

"Lots of different people go," he said, smiling. "You don't have to like, view a dead body or anything." He grinned at her, so glad she was here, with him.

"Oh, well, I'll have to check my schedule," she said.

"Yeah, I know," he said. "While you're at it, check and see if you have time to go parasailing tomorrow."

"Tomorrow?"

"They do tours all the way until eight o'clock," he said. "And Sierra's been bugging me to go, and I thought we'd all like to go."

Lisa searched his face, and he wasn't sure what she was thinking. "I've always wanted to go parasailing on a date," she said. "I'm in."

Cal's face split into a grin. "Tell me what time to book the tour."

————

THE FOLLOWING EVENING, CAL WAITED ON THE DOCK FOR Lisa. He, Sierra, Mikel had already been fitted for their harnesses, and the tour wasn't set to go for another twenty minutes. She still had time to get there, but she was cutting it close.

And then he saw her, a high blonde ponytail on top of her head swinging as she hurried toward him. He lifted his hand, and she jogged a few steps. She looked happy and carefree in a pair of white sandals and a sundress that the breeze played with.

"Hey," he said, his heart suddenly fuller than it had ever been. "You look great." He hugged her and led her down the dock to the parasailing hut. "They just need to fit you for a harness. She's here," he said to the kid working the booth.

After she was ready, Cal put his hand on the small of her back as she climbed onto the boat. "Back here," Sierra said, and Lisa went to her left to the two open seats at the back of the boat.

"I'm not so sure about this," she said, eyeing the equipment on the back of the boat.

"Right?" Sierra said. "I literally just said the same thing to Mikel here."

"I said they take people out on boats like this all the time," the teenager said. "It's going to be fine."

Cal sat next to Lisa, a little nervous himself. But before he knew it, the boat's engine roared to life and they started moving away from the dock. Cal loved being out on the open water, and he smiled as he tipped his head toward the sun and let the wind whip through his hair.

Lisa whooped too, and Cal was so glad he was here with her, experiencing this. Making new memories outside of the walls of his home, with a woman he really liked.

He lifted his arm around her, and she leaned into him

as she pressed her sunhat onto her head so the wind wouldn't steal it.

"All right," the boat captain said several minutes later. "Who's going first?" He looked between Cal and Sierra, and no one said anything.

"We are," Lisa said, standing up and pulling her sundress over her head to reveal a black one-piece swimming suit. Cal's mouth went dry, and it wasn't because he was about to strap himself to a seat and fly behind a boat.

Or maybe it was partly because of that.

"Yeah," he said, his heart pounding hard. "We are." He stepped where the captain told him, strapped himself in, let the assistant check everything, and then he gave Sierra a thumbs-up. "This is going to be great," he said, trying to assure himself as well as everyone else on the boat.

"Here we go," the captain said, and Cal didn't really have a chance to take a deep breath before the boat took off.

His yell matched Lisa's scream as they sailed up and behind the boat. She laughed, and he did too, his stomach somewhere down at the bottom of his feet. And then…then, the most beautiful view of the ocean and the island of Getaway Bay spread before him.

"Wow," he said, reaching over to take Lisa's hand in his. "This is amazing." Now that they were up and the line was out, it felt like he was floating, the clear, crisp ocean air rising up to meet him.

"So amazing," Lisa confirmed.

Cal tore his eyes from the glorious view of blue water and tan sand and green trees and looked at Lisa. "Thanks for coming with me."

"Thanks for inviting me." She grinned at him, and the seat swooped, causing another shriek to come from her throat.

Cal started laughing, everything in him tingling, either from the sudden drop or the fact that he and Lisa were here together, parasailing.

He hoped it was the parasailing.

Chapter Twenty-One

A couple of weeks later, Lisa sat next to Cal, his hand gripped tightly in hers as a woman talked about the death of her son. She wept, and she wasn't the only one. Lisa had sucked back her own tears a half-dozen times, and she didn't even know any of these people.

Yet there was a sense of family here among them. Lisa had never spent a Monday as well as she had this one, and the meeting wasn't even over yet.

No wonder Cal liked coming to these. They were full of good memories of dear people, and Lisa really liked thinking of them as still with their loved ones here on Earth.

When the meeting ended—Cal hadn't said a word—they stood and started chatting with the Chief of Police of all people. Lisa liked Chief Gardner, and they'd chitchatted a little bit about how his daughter was doing before the meeting.

"Oh, I see why you like coming to these," Lisa said when she spied the platter of doughnuts on a nearby table.

"Yeah, the refreshments aren't bad," Cal said, selecting a chocolate frosted doughnut. "I haven't eaten lunch yet, so this'll probably make me sick." He took a big bite anyway and looked over her shoulder. He nodded toward someone, and Lisa turned.

"Hey, so, uh." The Chief shifted his feet and lifted his hat to put it on. "Do you know if Deirdre Bernard is seeing anyone?"

Surprise shot right to Lisa's vocal cords. The Chief had his eye on Deirdre?

"No," she blurted. "No, she sure isn't."

"Great, thank you."

"We should set up a double date," Lisa said, her mind racing down an exciting path right now.

Cal coughed, and the Chief actually barked the word, "No."

"No double date?" She looked back and forth between the two men, almost giving herself whiplash.

"No setting up," the Chief said. "I can get my own date when I'm ready." He nodded to Lisa and then Cal before striding out of the room, sans doughnut.

"Wow, okay," Lisa said, feeling giddy for her friend. "He and Deirdre."

"He said they'd been out before," he said. "Didn't

work out for some reason." Cal finished his doughnut. "Do you have time for lunch?"

"Yeah, we're meeting Riley and Evan, remember?"

"Oh, right." Cal had obviously not remembered, but he smiled at her and laced his fingers through hers. "That bistro you girls love, right?"

"Right. And you'll like it too. They have these Hawaiian spam rolls that have your name all over them."

"Lead on," he said, chuckling, and Lisa did just that.

"Thanks for inviting me to this," she said. "I learned a lot."

"Yeah," Cal said with a sigh. "It's not a bad way to spend a lunch hour."

"Spending time with you is always a good time," Lisa said, realizing too late how much she'd revealed.

Cal paused and looked at her, his feelings right there in his expression too. "I like spending time with you too, Lisa." He bent down and kissed her, the sweetest kiss of her life. Lisa sighed into his touch, realizing that she could easily fall for this man in a matter of days.

In fact, she'd already started the slide in that direction.

———

Six months later:

"Wow," Lisa said, gazing up at all the trees. Even in the winter, the rainforest was beautiful. "I can't believe you have a place out here. It feels so remote."

209

"We've been off the road for two minutes," Cal said with a laugh. "And the beach is right behind us."

Lisa didn't look behind her. She was too entranced with the emerald green foliage, the brilliant blue sky, all of it. A house emerged from out of the branches, and Lisa pulled in a breath. "Is that it? It's awesome."

"It's practically a hut," Cal said, but Lisa knew he loved this place. He'd come a few times over the past six months without her, and she hadn't pressed him to invite her. He would when he was ready. "Jo and I fell in love with it when we first saw it."

"I can see why." Lisa admired the bright blue exterior, with the bright white shutters. The porch spanned the whole front of it, and the rocking chairs looked like a great place to waste an afternoon with this man at her side. The front door was a pale yellow, and everything looked as charming as could be.

"There's indoor plumbing," he said. "And the boat is in the shed behind the house."

"Kitchen?"

"Very small," he said. "Everything about it is very small, Lise."

She loved it when he used her nickname, and she basked in the love she felt for Cal. She'd told him she loved him; he'd said it back. They'd enjoyed the last six months together, and Lisa was looking forward to many more months of happiness with him.

No, he hadn't asked her to marry him, and they hadn't even really talked about marriage all that much.

He had a now-fifteen-year-old, and she wasn't sure if he wanted more children or not.

He pulled the truck to a stop and got out, waiting for her to join him. "So this place has two bedrooms and a bathroom. Jo and I would just come for a quick weekend away, and we brought Sierra a few times when she was little. The beach is a half a mile away, and we walk through the trees to get there." He mounted the steps and looked at the rocking chairs to his right.

"I built those, and I'll build you one so you have your own to sit in when we come." He smiled and opened the front door.

Lisa's heart felt like it might burst. "Do you carry the boat down to the beach every time you go fishing?"

"I dock it down there," he said. "I nailed a spike into the sand, and nobody bothers it."

"Not a lot of people out here."

"There's about a dozen huts like this one," he said. "So no, not a lot. I know most of them, and they know my boat. We watch out for each other."

Everything about this little house and the vacation community up here by Lightning Point sounded wonderful to Lisa.

"So here's the main room," he said. "Kitchen is right against the back wall there. Two-burner stove, fridge, microwave, small sink."

The space held one couch and had windows everywhere. The walls were stark white, and the place seemed filled with light.

"Two bedrooms over here," he said, indicating the doors. "And a bathroom in the back. There's no laundry facility. If we get super dirty, we just hose off in the back yard."

"Cold," Lisa said. She grabbed onto Cal's arm with both of her hands and hugged it. "I *love* this place. Thanks for inviting me up here. I know this place is special for you." She gazed at him while he looked around at this house he clearly loved.

"It is," he said. "And now we can start making our own memories here." He faced her, a bright light in his eye that made Lisa's pulse blip a little faster through her body. "All right, let's bring in our food, and we can get down to the beach whenever you're ready."

She worked side-by-side with him as they brought in their bags of groceries and a cooler. She hauled in her rolling suitcase and put it in the bedroom closest to the front door. They'd be out here for a few days, and when she got back to Getaway Bay, she'd only have a few days until Riley's wedding.

Everything was going to be perfect for her best friend, and Lisa hadn't had so much fun planning a wedding in a very long time. Or maybe everything at work had seemed easier because she'd had Cal in her life all these months.

She changed into her swimming suit and double-checked her beach bag for sunscreen. After donning her sun hat, she went into the main room and said, "Time for the beach."

Cal looked up from his phone, his eyes traveling the length of her body and back to her eyes. "I can see that." He stood and came toward her, which meant he took two steps before he gathered her into his arms. "I love you."

Lisa smiled up at him, thrilled with how and when he chose to express his feelings. "I love you, too, Cal." She snuggled into his chest. "I have been thinking, what with Riley getting married soon and all of that...."

"Oh, yeah?" he prompted, obviously in no hurry to head out to the beach. In fact, he started to sway as if they were dancing right there in his tiny living room.

"Yeah," she said. "Do you see yourself getting married again?"

"Yes," he whispered.

Lisa's pulse pranced through her chest at the same time a smile exploded onto her face. "No rush or anything, honestly. We just haven't talked about it at all."

"No rush," he echoed.

Lisa straightened and looked into his eyes. "And one more hard question before we go to the beach. And you can take some time to think about it. I know you like time to think when I ask you hard questions."

"Depends on the question," Cal said.

She bent to pick up her beach bag. "This one's about kids. I love Sierra to death. I'm fine if that's all the family you want. Honestly, I am. But have you ever thought... do you think we'll have kids together?"

Cal blinked, and Lisa could see she had surprised him with the question. She waited, the silence between them comfortable now. There had been some months that had felt incredibly slow to Lisa. And some times where their relationship picked up steam overnight.

She'd realized that not every day could be one lived with the gas pedal pressed all the way to the floor. In fact, the slower drive days were just as savory and some of her favorites.

"I think…I would like more kids," Cal said slowly.

Lisa grinned at him, feeling playful and strong and sexy all at the same time. "You know what that means, don't you, Cal?"

"What?"

"You better ask me to marry you—soon." She flipped her hair over her shoulder and headed for the back door. "And bring your muscles, because I'm not going to be able to help with the boat."

He laughed, following her. He did carry the boat down to the beach, and Lisa kept exclaiming about the flowers and the plants growing on either side of the path.

"It really is the jungle here," she said. And then she took a step, and the beach spread before her. "Oh, wow. I want to move here."

Cal just laughed and kept moving. He finally flipped the boat over and dropped it to the sand when he was on the wet, hard-packed part of the beach. "You can't move here," he said. "The commute is too long. And didn't you hear the part about how the house has no laundry facilities?"

Lisa dropped her beach bag and spread her arms

wide, letting the energy of this untouched part of Getaway Bay flow through her. She sighed as she closed her eyes, this moment so surreal and so wonderful.

When she looked at Cal again, he just stood there watching her. "But there's you, baby," she said. "And you definitely seem like the type of man who knows how to wash clothes by hand." She tiptoed her fingers up his chest and curled both hands around his neck.

She leaned her forehead against his, pure joy moving through her. Contentment. Neither of them said anything. They didn't need to.

This memory would be with her forever, and she just wanted to bask in it.

Chapter Twenty-Two

C al rowed himself and Lisa out to the reef and taught her how to put her pole over the side. "I can't believe you've lived here your whole life and have never been fishing," he said, smiling at her.

"Oh, well, I mean, I've been."

"You said you hadn't." He looked at her as he baited his hook.

"I meant in many years. Or as an adult. My dad took us when we were little." She held her pole like she expected it to grow wings and fly away. "And I liked catching the fish, but I didn't want to clean them. Dad said once that the next fish we caught, we'd have to gut it. I stopped going after that." She shrugged one shoulder and smiled. "Not one for guts, I guess."

"I guess not," Cal said. "Cleaning the fish isn't my favorite thing either. I don't normally catch a whole lot anyway." He set his pole and leaned back with a sigh.

"It's more about the experience. The time on the water. In the boat."

"I love the boat," she said.

"I made this one," Cal said. "It's father-approved." A sense of pride filled Cal. These past several months had been so...cleansing for him. He loved working with his hands, and he'd decided he didn't want his father's legacy to fade into oblivion. So in addition to being there for Sierra, maintaining his construction business, and advancing his relationship with Lisa, he'd started learning how to build fishing boats from his father. The work had been rewarding in a way Cal hadn't anticipated, and his father had just gotten another order for a boat that Cal would be building solo.

"Christmas with your mom," he said next, because he had something else to ask Lisa and he couldn't quite get the words in the right order.

"Yes," she said. "The sisters. Everyone." She looked at him, though it was hard to tell with the sun hat and sunglasses covering her eyes. "And we're having a nice dinner at your house, with just Sierra on Christmas Eve."

"Yes," he said. "And we can go see my brothers and parents the day after." He was tired just thinking about all the visiting. But Lisa and Sierra got along great, and they could carry a conversation if he didn't feel like talking.

"And then on the twenty-seventh, we can come here and enjoy the silence." She grinned at him, and Cal was grateful she knew him well enough to know he'd need a day of detoxing after all the holidays. "But you're okay to come to Riley's wedding with me, right?"

"Of course." He cleared his throat. "And speaking of weddings...." He reached down and unzipped a pocket in his backpack. "How do you feel about starting to plan our wedding?" He pulled out a black box and cracked the lid, the sunlight glinting on the diamond ring inside.

"Oh, my word," Lisa said, her voice mostly made of air.

"I love you, Lisa," Cal said. "I want you to be able to come home to me and Sierra after a long day of wedding planning. I want to come home to you. Will you marry me?"

She laughed, quickly cutting off the sound as she covered her mouth with her hand. She nodded, and Cal smiled. "You gotta say it, sweetheart."

"Yes," she said. "Yes, I'll marry you."

He tipped forward and kissed her, a sloppy one because she was still giggling. "Oh, my goodness," she kept saying as he slipped the ring onto her finger. "Cal, this is a beautiful ring." She held her hand out and stared at it. "I love you."

He kissed her again, holding her close to him. "Sierra helped me pick it out."

"I love it." She beamed at him. "I can't believe this. I wasn't expecting...." She laughed again. "When were you thinking?"

"That's up to you," he said. "I just need you to show up, but I'm guessing you have a file somewhere in your office with all the things you want for your dream wedding."

"I do not," she said, but she immediately shook her head. "Wait. I totally do." She laughed again, and Cal joined in this time. "I want to get married in the summer. I've always wanted that. Maybe July or August? That gives me seven or eight months."

"Perfect," Cal said. "Whatever you want, sweetheart. Maybe not when school is on."

"So before school," Lisa said, looking out over the ocean. "I can do that."

"Will you dance with me at our wedding?" he asked. Their eyes met, and Lisa nodded slowly.

"Yes," she said. "Dancing should definitely be part of our wedding."

Chapter Twenty-Three

L isa could not believe her wedding day had arrived. She'd spent so many long years wondering if she'd ever be the bride and not the wedding planner—and today was that day.

"Sweetie," her mother said, opening her bedroom door. "Oh, good, you're awake. It's time to start getting ready. Ash will be here in an hour with the dress. Riley's just texted to say she's on her way, and Shannon said she'd be here by nine."

"I'm up." Lisa smiled at her mother. She showered and heard voices down the hall in her kitchen. Dressed in her undergarments and a fluffy white robe she'd bought just for this day, she padded down the hall to find Riley and Shannon sipping coffee with her mother.

"There she is," Shannon said, jumping to her feet. "Our bride." She hugged Lisa, who embraced her back.

"Thank you so much," Lisa said. "Now I know how

brides feel about us." She hugged Riley too, who held her extra tight for an extra long time. When she pulled away, they were both a little teary, and Lisa hadn't expected to feel anything but happiness.

"I love you guys," she said. "It's been so great being your friend. And thank you for being my friend."

"Love you," Riley said, wiping her eyes. "And now I'm going to need someone to redo my makeup."

"Better start on that," Shannon said. "Carole will be here in fifteen minutes, and then Ash will want to do a final fitting on the dress." Her phone chimed, and she reached for it. "I'm heading down to the beach, where Charlotte is setting up the altar." She flashed a smile at Riley and Lisa. "I'll see you down there. No later than eleven-thirty, right?"

"Right," Riley said, and she was extremely anal about weddings starting on time. "I'll make sure she's there on time." She opened her makeup kit, and Lisa sat down at the table. Her mother put a cup of coffee in front of her, and Riley turned on some calming music before she started sweeping the makeup brush across Lisa's face.

Lisa kept her emotions tightly contained so she wouldn't ruin her best friend's work, and she hugged Carole when she arrived. She started drying Lisa's hair into perfectly straight locks, and then she pulled it all to the top of Lisa's head to create an elegant topknot.

Ash arrived, and Lisa stepped into the dress she'd had designed. It fit perfectly, but Ash wasn't satisfied with a seam in the back. She ran out to her car to grab her portable sewing machine and set up shop at the other end of the table.

Carole added jewels and ribbons to Lisa's hair—Lisa's version of a veil—while Ash sewed and Riley finished with the final touches on Lisa's makeup.

She finally stepped into the dress and the shoes and everything was in place.

"Oh, Grandma's earrings," her mother said, opening the small drawer beside Lisa's refrigerator. She put them on for Lisa and pulled her into another tight hug. "You're beautiful. Cal is so lucky."

Lisa felt like the lucky one, but she just nodded. "Okay, get me to the beach," she said, eyeing the clock. "We don't have much time."

The temperature at the end of July on the beach was brutal, but Lisa had ordered fans and misters to keep the area for guests cool. People had already arrived, some in their seats, some walking through the sand to the large, white tent that had been set up for the ceremony. Cal had carved the altar out of one of the trees surrounding the cabin up by Lightning Point, and Lisa had ordered the roses and tulips she'd wanted for so long. They'd cover the top, where a candle would burn.

Not a real one, as Lisa had plenty of experience with the ocean breezes ruining her best laid plans. She'd switched to using tall, beautiful candles that had fake flames, and they were just as amazing as the real thing.

"We're getting pictures of everything, right?" she

asked Riley as she caught a glimpse of the huge yellow bows on the backs of the chairs, who nodded.

"Aiden's been here for an hour," she said. "He'll have all the detail shots, and he'll get everything during the ceremony." She led Lisa into the staging building, only a dozen or so yards from the outdoor ceremony. Riley brushed something invisible from Lisa's shoulder, pushing the thin strap back into place. "You're beautiful, and this is going to be the best wedding of the year."

Lisa nodded, and Riley added, "I have to go check on a couple of things. You stay here."

Lisa was familiar with this part of the wedding. She'd wait in this room until it was time to begin. Then Cal's daughter would walk her down the aisle, where her future husband and love of her life waited.

And then...she'd be Mrs. Cal Lewiston.

Finally.

Lisa's tears gathered in her eyes again, but she blinked them back. She wasn't going to worry about who hadn't come—her father. She wasn't going to wish for things she didn't have, because she had *so* much. So, so much.

"Ready?" Riley asked, and Lisa spun toward her. Time had passed in a blink, and Lisa nodded. Sierra stepped passed Riley, and she looked absolutely radiant in the pale pink dress that mirrored Lisa's. Well, as closely as it could, as Lisa had had her dress designed, and they'd had to buy Sierra's from a shop.

But the two dresses had the same ruffled fabric over

the bodice and down the stomach, and they both laced in the back until a zipper took over near the waistline.

"You're beautiful," Lisa said, taking Sierra into her arms. "Thank you so much for giving me your father."

"Thank you for taking him," Sierra said, squeezing Lisa tight.

She pulled back and held Sierra by the shoulders. "I love having you as a daughter."

Sierra smiled and nodded, her eyes glassy. "You're going to be a good mother."

"We're all going to be late," Riley said. "And the cake is melting."

"Okay." Lisa took a big breath and linked her arm through Riley's. "We're ready." They left the staging building, and someone behind the scenes changed the music. Everyone stood and turned toward her and Sierra, whose step faltered.

Lisa kept them moving, her goal singular—the man at the end of the aisle, waiting by the custom altar he'd built for them. He smiled at her and Sierra as they continued to step toward him, and he first hugged Sierra when they arrived.

"Love you," he whispered, and she went to sit beside one of her uncles. He took Lisa's hand and grinned at her. "And wow. Look at you."

Lisa felt loved and cherished, and she beamed right back at him. "And you, Mister Lewiston. I don't think I've ever seen you wear a tie."

He chuckled, shook his head, and turned toward the

altar. Lisa admired it, running her fingertips along the edge of the wood peeking out from beneath the flowers. She met Cal's eye again, and then they looked at the pastor together.

Together, just like Lisa wanted to do everything with this man. Raise a teenager. Have a baby. Build a home.

Together.

When it was her turn to say I do, she did in a loud voice, and she kissed Cal with everything she had. They turned to the clapping crowd and lifted their joined hands, and Lisa took the first step of the rest of her life with the man she loved.

Together.

———

There's another bride coming to Getaway Bay! Read on to meet Deirdre - a consultant at Your Tidal Forever - and Wyatt in **THE ISLAND WEDDING!**

Sneak Peek! The Island Wedding
Chapter One

W yatt Gardner sat in his police cruiser, watching person after person walk down the sidewalk in front of him. Most of them were women, and they were dressed nicely, with wedges and pumps and skirts, so he knew they were going to the September Sandy Singles event.

That was why he'd driven from the police station to the community center, too. He just couldn't quite get himself to get out of the car. Yet.

But he was going to get out. He was going to go in. He was going to put himself out there again. Try to find someone that he could spend the rest of his life with. He was only forty-four years old. He had a lot of life to live yet.

With Jennifer out of the house completely now, married and living her best life, Wyatt had plenty of time and money to move on. Plus, he really wanted to do the same thing his daughter had done. Find someone to love as completely as she had.

He'd been working for the Getaway Bay Police Department for twenty-three years now, and he was seriously thinking about hanging up his hat. Permanently.

But the thought of sitting around his house all day, nothing to do…he couldn't even imagine that, and that kept him getting up every morning, running along the beach, and going into the station.

"Going in," he said, as if he were letting his crew know at the station so they could send back-up if he didn't check in soon. He got out of the car and looked both ways down the sidewalk. But everyone would know where he was going and why he'd come the moment he stepped inside.

Wyatt held his head high and nodded to another man as he approached. He didn't know the guy, but most people in Getaway Bay knew Wyatt. So he nodded and stepped in line with him. "Can I go in with you?"

"Of course, Chief." The other guy gave him a smile, and they went through the marked door so other patrons of the community center who weren't attending the singles event could still use the facilities.

"What's your name?" he asked the man.

"Henry Bishop," he said.

"Nice to meet you, Henry." They met a line, and Wyatt slowed to join it. He wasn't particularly good with small talk, but he'd had plenty of practice over the years. "What do you do?"

"I'm a surfing instructor," he said. "Own a little hut in East Bay."

"Oh, that's great," Wyatt said. "I love surfing."

Henry smiled at him again, and a couple of women in front of them turned around. "I've used your surfing lessons," one of them said. "They were good."

"Yeah?" Henry asked. "Who was your instructor?"

"I can't remember." She twirled a lock of her dark hair around her ear. "Do you give lessons?"

"Of course, yeah," Henry said with a smile. "You didn't learn the first time?"

The brunette shrugged. "It's been a while, and I think I'm ready to get back in the water."

Wyatt was pretty sure her comment was some sort of euphemism he didn't understand, and he simply stood outside the trio as they continued to chat about surfing lessons and the best places to catch the biggest waves.

He entered last behind them, not catching either woman's name as they moved ahead of him. The scent of coconuts and suntan oil met his nose when he entered the room after logging his name with the clerk standing at the door.

This singles event was a free couple of hours on a Friday night, and with summer in full swing, Wyatt had decided now was a great time to branch out of his usual find-a-date tactics. That honestly wasn't hard, because he currently had no tactics to find a date. Most of the women he came in contact with were under arrest or employees. The department didn't have rules against relationships among co-workers, as long as all the proper paperwork was filed. But Wyatt had never wanted to be with a fellow cop.

Piper had been his complete opposite in every way, and he'd loved her with everything in him. When she'd died, a piece of Wyatt had died too.

For a while there, he'd thought it was the most important part of himself. But through his grief counseling, and with the passage of time, he'd learned that he still had the capacity to love. He'd seen friends move past difficult divorces, as well as the loss of loved ones. One of his good friends from their grief meetings had just gotten married, and Wyatt had been spurred by Cal's example to find his own date.

Tonight, he told himself as he surveyed the room. The cop inside him couldn't help checking for all the exits and looking around for a safe place to hide should something happen. He estimated the number of people in the room to be about one hundred, and the vast majority of them were women.

Wyatt supposed he should be happy about that, but all he felt was pressure. A lot of pressure. He could get a phone number tonight from someone who wasn't really that interested in him. She might only talk to him, because there weren't that many other men to choose from.

He took a deep breath, stepped over to the refreshment table, which was smartly placed by the entrance, and grabbed a plastic cup of punch. With something to occupy his attention, he took a drink and surveyed the groups of women closest to him. He'd been under the impression there would be structured activities during the Sandy Singles event, but if so, they hadn't started yet.

He'd taken one step when someone came over the microphone. "All right, everyone. We're about to start our first speed-dating activity. I need all women on the left side of the room. All the men on the right. That's right. Women on the left. Men on the right."

Wyatt followed the directions, and he'd been right. Only about twenty-five percent of the attendees were men, and he hoped the organizer of these activities knew what to do with the extra women.

"We're going to divide the women into three groups," the woman at the mic said. "Men, I hope you have a drink nearby and are ready to chat." She beamed at the right side of the room, and Wyatt swallowed his nerves.

He was good at talking to strangers. He could make someone he suspected of heinous crimes talk to him, trust him, connect with him. A woman was somehow harder, but he pushed his nerves away.

He didn't want to live the next thirty years alone. Or even another one.

So he put a smile on his face, took the seat he was given, and prepared himself to talk to people for the next couple of hours.

A woman with dirty blonde hair sat in front of him, her blue eyes sparkling like sunlight off the ocean. Her hair was all piled up on top of her head like she'd walked into the event from off the beach, and Wyatt smiled at her.

Not his type.

But he could be nice. "I'm Wyatt Gardner," he said, extending his hand.

"Everyone knows who you are," she said with a smile. She put her hand in his and cocked her head. "I'm Bridgette Baker."

"Nice to meet you," he said, thinking he was a better liar than he'd like to be. The small talk was small with Bridgette, and when the bell rang, the women got up and moved down a seat. Wyatt looked to his right, realizing he had a very long night ahead of him.

After five rounds of speed-dating, he'd taken two slips of paper from women he would not be calling, and he got to his feet when the organizer said, "Five-minute break, and then we'll start with the second group of women."

Yeah, Wyatt wouldn't be. He'd thought this Sandy Singles even was a good idea, and he was willing to admit it when he was wrong.

He headed for the door, not caring how many people saw him. The whole island knew about Piper's death, and they'd just assume he was still too broken up over her death to date. Or they'd speculate that he'd gotten an emergency call. In fact, he pulled out his phone and looked at it, tapping as if sending a text to someone very important.

In truth, the only place he needed to be was on his

couch, a really great fish taco in his hands, and the television lulling him to sleep.

Pathetic, maybe. But right now, Wyatt was okay with that.

In his peripheral vision, he caught sight of someone directly in front of him. Someone he was about to run into. He looked up at the same time he collided with the woman, who obviously hadn't been watching where she was going either.

"Oof," she said, and to Wyatt's great horror, she fell backward. Her eyes widened, and she cried out as she fell in super-slow motion. Wyatt tried to reach for her, but she flailed out of his reach. Way out of his reach, because he'd just bowled over Deirdre Bernard.

She hit the ground, and everything that had slowed down raced forward again. "Deirdre," Wyatt said, his voice mostly air. He hurried over to her and knelt down. "I'm so sorry." He didn't quite know where to put his hands.

His brain screamed at him to do something helpful. *Apologize. Say you're ready.*

He just hovered above Deirdre, his memories streaming through him now. Memories of the relationship they'd tried. The things she'd said to him when they'd broken up. All of those were true, and Deirdre deserved some credit for Wyatt's reappearance at the grief meetings on the island.

Their eyes met, and Wyatt put his hands at his sides. "Are you okay?"

"I'm okay," she said, and Wyatt wanted to smooth her hair, tuck the errant locks behind her ear, and apologize for not being ready last time.

Could there be a *this* time?

"Let me help you," he said, giving her his hand and helping her stand up. "Sorry, I wasn't watching where I was going."

"I wasn't either." She smoothed down her blouse and looked at Wyatt fully again. "Look at us, running into each other. Literally." Deirdre smiled, and Wyatt remembered how beautiful she was when she did. His heartbeat accelerated, and he definitely wanted a second chance with this woman.

"What are you doing right now?" he asked boldly.

"Right this second?"

"Yeah."

She looked over her shoulder toward the room he'd just exited. "Well, there's this singles event a couple of my girlfriends came to. I've been waiting in the car, and —" She gave a light laugh. "I finally decided to come in."

"I was just headed out, and I'm starving. Do you want to grab some dinner?"

"With you?"

"Yes," Wyatt said, hoping she wouldn't say no. How humiliating would that be?

Deirdre narrowed her eyes slightly and seemed to peer directly into his soul. "Wyatt, you're a great man. But I don't...it didn't work last time, and I don't think it's going to work this time." She patted his bicep as she stepped around him.

Wyatt turned, speechless, and watched her enter the Sandy Singles event room.

What a disaster. Swallowing back his embarrassment, Wyatt held his head as high as he could as he walked out of the community center and back to his cruiser.

There weren't enough fish tacos on the planet to erase this night from his memory.

———

Oh no. Deirdre and Wyatt don't seem to be off to a good start. **Read THE ISLAND WEDDING today!**

Books in the Getaway Bay Romance series

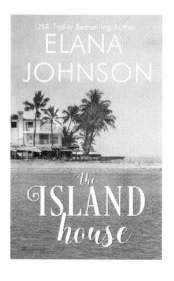

The Island House (Book 1): Charlotte Madsen's whole world came crashing down six months ago with the words, "I met someone else."

Can Charlotte navigate the healing process to find love again?

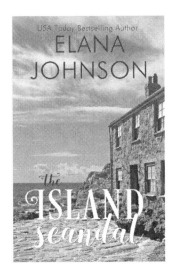

The Island Scandal (Book 2): Ashley Fox has known three things since age twelve: she was an excellent seamstress, what her wedding would look like, and that she'd never leave the island of Getaway Bay. Now, at age 35, she's been right about two of them, at least.

Can Burke and Ash find a way to navigate a romance when they've only ever been friends?

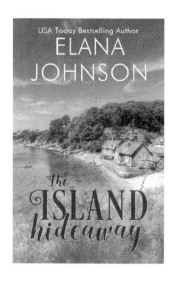

The Island Hideaway (Book 3): She's 37, single (except for the cat), and a synchronized swimmer looking to make some extra cash. Pathetic, right? She thinks so, and she's going to spend this summer housesitting a cliffside hideaway and coming up with a plan to turn her life around.

Can Noah and Zara fight their feelings for each other as easily as they trade jabs? Or will this summer shape up to be the one that provides the romance they've each always wanted?

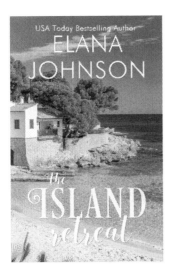

The Island Retreat (Book 4): Shannon's 35, divorced, and the highlight of her day is getting to the coffee shop before the morning rush. She tells herself that's fine, because she's got two cats and a past filled with emotional abuse. But she might be ready to heal so she can retreat into the arms of a man she's known for years...

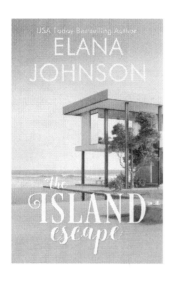

The Island Escape (Book 5): Riley Randall has spent eight years smiling at new brides, being excited for her friends as they find Mr. Right, and dating by a strict set of rules that she never breaks. But she might have to consider bending those rules ever so slightly if she wants an escape from the island...

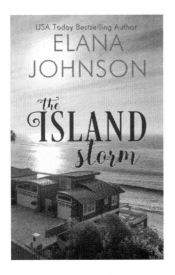

The Island Storm (Book 6): Lisa is 36, tired of the dating scene in Getaway Bay, and practically the only wedding planner at her company that hasn't found her own happy-ever-after. She's tried dating apps and blind dates...but could the company party put a man she's known for years into the spotlight?

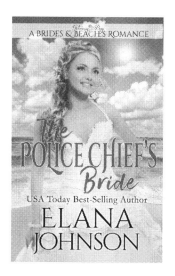

The Island Wedding (Book 7): Deirdre is almost 40, estranged from her teenaged daughter, and determined not to feel sorry for herself. She does the best she can with the cards life has dealt her and she's dreaming of another island wedding...but it certainly can't happen with the widowed Chief of Police.

Books in the Getaway Bay Resort Romance series

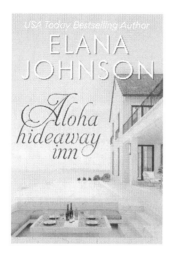

Aloha Hideaway Inn (Book 1): Can Stacey and the Aloha Hideaway Inn survive strange summer weather, the arrival of the new resort, *and* the start of a special relationship?

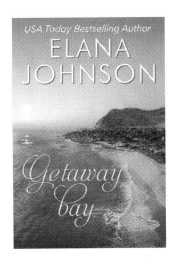

Getaway Bay (Book 2): Can Esther deal with dozens of business tasks, unhappy tourists, *and* the twists and turns in her new relationship?

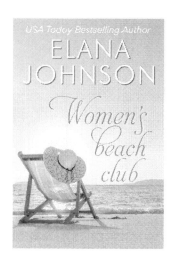

Women's Beach Club (Book 3): With the help of her friends in the Beach Club, can Tawny solve the mystery, stay safe, and keep her man?

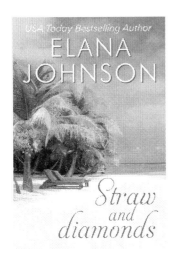

Straw and Diamonds (Book 4): Can Sasha maintain her sanity amidst their busy schedules, her issues with men like Jasper, and her desires to take her business to the next level?

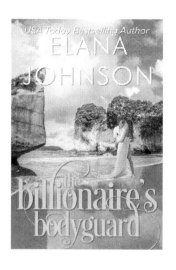

The Billionaire Club (Book 5): Can Lexie keep her business affairs in the shadows while she brings her relationship out of them? Or will she have to confess everything to her new friends...and Jason?

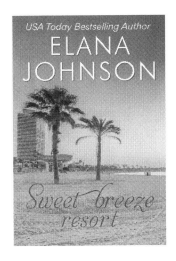

Sweet Breeze Resort (Book 6): Can Gina manage her business across the sea and finish the remodel at Sweet Breeze, all while developing a meaningful relationship with Owen and his sons?

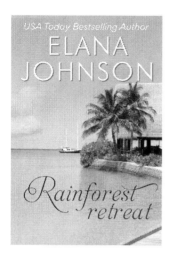

Rainforest Retreat (Book 7): As their paths continue to cross and Lawrence and Maizee spend more and more time together, will he find in her a retreat from all the family pressure? Can Maizee manage her relationship with her boss, or will she once again put her heart—and her job—on the line?

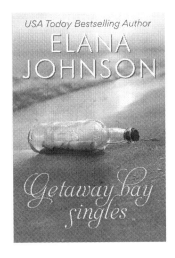

USA Today Bestselling Author
ELANA JOHNSON
Getaway bay singles

Getaway Bay Singles (Book 8): Can Katie bring him into her life, her daughter's life, and manage her business while he manages the app? Or will everything fall apart for a second time?

Books in the Stranded in Getaway Bay Romance series

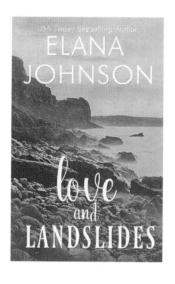

Love and Landslides (Book 1): A freak storm has her sliding down the mountain...right into the arms of her ex. As Eden and Holden spend time out in the wilds of Hawaii trying to survive, their old flame is rekindled. But with secrets and old feelings in the way, will Holden be able to take all the broken pieces of his life and put them back together in a way that makes sense? Or will he lose his heart and the reputation of his company because of a single landslide?

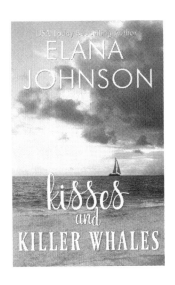

Kisses and Killer Whales (Book 2): Friends who ditch her. A pod of killer whales. A limping cruise ship. All reasons Iris finds herself stranded on an deserted island with the handsome Navy SEAL...

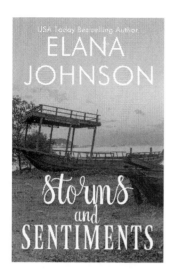

Storms and Sentiments (Book 3): He can throw a precision pass, but he's dead in the water in matters of the heart...

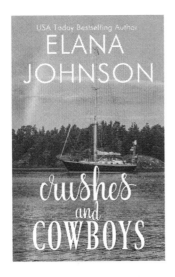

Crushes and Cowboys (Book 4): Tired of the dating scene, a cowboy billionaire puts up an Internet ad to find a woman to come out to a deserted island with him to see if they can make a love connection...

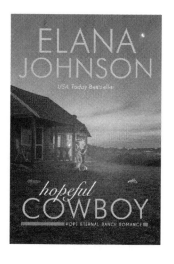

Hopeful Cowboy, Book 1:
Can Ginger and Nate find
their happily-ever-after, keep
up their duties on the ranch,
and build a family? Or will the
risk be too great for them
both?

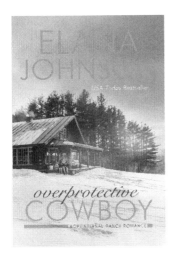

Overprotective Cowboy, Book 2: Can Ted and Emma face their pasts so they can truly be ready to step into the future together? Or will everything between them fall apart once the truth comes out?

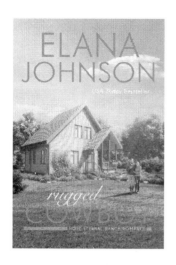

Rugged Cowboy, Book 3: He's a cowboy mechanic with two kids and an ex-wife on the run. She connects better to horses than humans. Can Dallas and Jess find their way to each other at Hope Eternal Ranch?

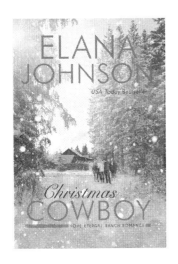

Christmas Cowboy, Book 4: He needs to start a new story for his life. She's dealing with a lot of family issues. This Christmas, can Slate and Jill find solace in each other at Hope Eternal Ranch?

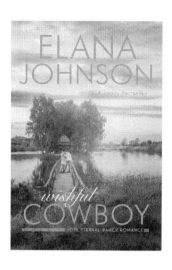

Wishful Cowboy, Book 5: He needs somewhere to belong. She has a heart as wide as the Texas sky. Can Luke and Hannah find their one true love in each other?

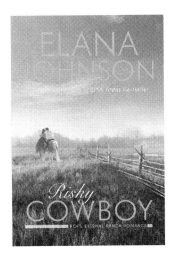

Risky Cowboy, Book 6: She's tired of making cheese and ice cream on her family's dairy farm, but when the cowboy hired to replace her turns out to be an ex-boyfriend, Clarissa suddenly isn't so sure about leaving town... Will Spencer risk it all to convince Clarissa to stay and give him a second chance?

Books in the Hawthorne Harbor Romance
series

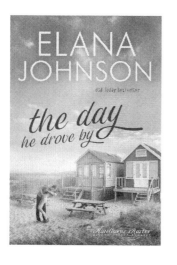

**The Day He Drove By
(Hawthorne Harbor
Second Chance Romance,
Book 1):** A widowed florist,
her ten-year-old daughter, and
the paramedic who delivered
the girl a decade earlier...

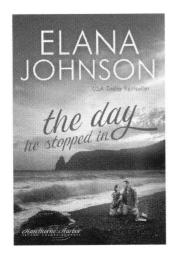

The Day He Stopped In (Hawthorne Harbor Second Chance Romance, Book 2): Janey Germaine is tired of entertaining tourists in Olympic National Park all day and trying to keep her twelve-year-old son occupied at night. When longtime friend and the Chief of Police, Adam Herrin, offers to take the boy on a ride-along one fall evening, Janey starts to see him in a different light. Do they have the courage to take their relationship out of the friend zone?

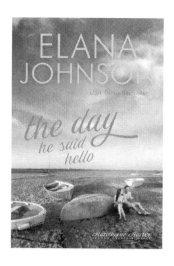

The Day He Said Hello (Hawthorne Harbor Second Chance Romance, Book 3): Bennett Patterson is content with his boring firefighting job and his big great dane...until he comes face-toface with his high school girlfriend, Jennie Zimmerman, who swore she'd never return to Hawthorne Harbor. Can they rekindle their old flame? Or will their opposite personalities keep them apart?

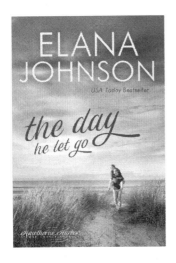

The Day He Let Go (Hawthorne Harbor Second Chance Romance, Book 4): Trent Baker is ready for another relationship, and he's hopeful he can find someone who wants him and to be a mother to his son. Lauren Michaels runs her own general contract company, and she's never thought she has a maternal bone in her body. But when she gets a second chance with the handsome K9 cop who blew her off when she first came to town, she can't say no... Can Trent and Lauren make their differences into strengths and build a family?

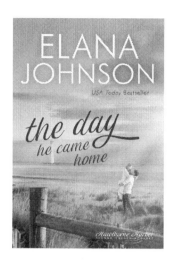

The Day He Came Home (Hawthorne Harbor Second Chance Romance, Book 5): A wounded Marine returns to Hawthorne Harbor years after the woman he was married to for exactly one week before she got an annulment...and then a baby nine months later. Can Hunter and Alice make a family out of past heartache?

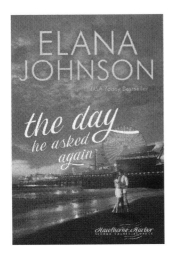

The Day He Asked Again (Hawthorne Harbor Second Chance Romance, Book 6): A Coast Guard captain would rather spend his time on the sea...unless he's with the woman he's been crushing on for months. Can Brooklynn and Dave make their second chance stick?

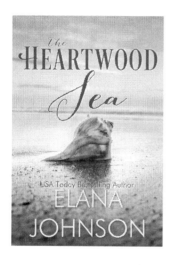

The Heartwood Sea (Book 1): She owns The Heartwood Inn. He needs the land the inn sits on to impress his boss. Neither one of them will give an inch. But will they give each other their hearts?

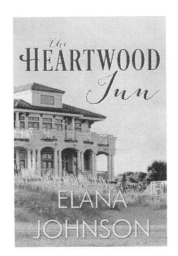

The Heartwood Inn (Book 2): She's excited to have a neighbor across the hall. He's got secrets he can never tell her. Will Olympia find a way to leave her past where it belongs so she can have a future with Chet?

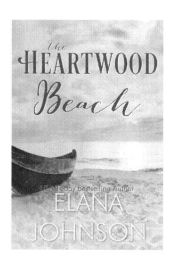

The Heartwood Beach (Book 3): She's got a stalker. He's got a loud bark. Can Sheryl tame her bodyguard into a boyfriend?

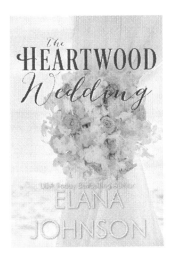

The Heartwood Wedding (Book 4): He needs a reason not to go out with a journalist. She'd like a guaranteed date for the summer. They don't get along, so keeping Brad in the not-her-real-fiancé category should be easy for Celeste. Totally easy.

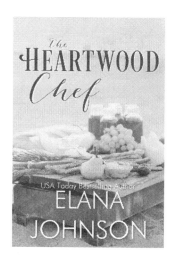

The Heartwood Chef (Book 5): They've been out before, and now they work in the same kitchen at The Heartwood Inn. Gwen isn't interested in getting anything filleted but fish, because Teagan's broken her heart before... Can Teagan and Gwen manage their professional relationship without letting feelings get in the way?

About Elana

Elana Johnson is the USA Today bestselling author of dozens of clean and wholesome contemporary romance novels. She lives in Utah, where she mothers two fur babies, taxis her daughter to theater several times a week, and eats a lot of Ferrero Rocher while writing. Find her on her website at elanajohnson.com.

Printed in Great Britain
by Amazon

62379430R00168